McCLINTOCK'S RELUCTANT BRIDE
By
Caroline Clemmons

McClintock's Reluctant Bride

Caroline Clemmons

Copyright 2015 Caroline Clemmons

ISBN-13: 978-1514790298

ISBN-10: 1514790297

Cover Graphics
Skye Moncrief

All rights reserved. Without limiting the rights under copyright reserved above, no part of this publication may be reproduced, stored in or introduced into a retrieval system or transmitted in any form or by any means (electronic, mechanical, photocopying, recording, or otherwise) without the prior written permission of both the copyright owner and the above publisher of this book.

Names, characters, places, and incidents are either the product of the author's imagination or are used fictitiously. Any resemblance to actual persons living or dead, businesses, events, or locales is purely coincidental.

Dear Reader,

Thank you for choosing my book from all the millions available. I love, love, love my readers and am so appreciative of your loyalty. I write for you. If ever you have comments or suggestions, I would love to hear them at mail to: caroline@carolineclemmons.com If you want to stay current on when I release a new book, please sign up for my newsletter. I hope you enjoy this book. If you do, please leave a review when you've finished at wherever you purchased the book.

Again, thank you,

Caroline

Chapter One

McClintock Falls, Texas, June 1886

Nettie Sue Clayton smiled at the antics of Josh McClintock and his equally inebriated friends. She didn't hold with drunkenness, but she supposed a single man's birthday was an acceptable occasion for revelry. She had a feeling that after tonight the handsome charmer would need a full day to recover.

"Happy Birthday to me! YeeHaw!" Josh held a beer above his head before lowering his arm to take a long swallow.

His friends let out a whoop loud enough to be heard for miles. The flock of adoring females surrounding Josh and his friends giggled. Nettie recognized a couple of the girls from church, but most were strangers. Her family had only recently moved here so she didn't yet know all the local residents.

At the back of Kathryn and Austin McClintock's sprawling two-story ranch home, the colorful lanterns strung from tree to tree swayed in the spring breeze. Couples twirled to lively tunes on the makeshift floor of wooden planking. Musicians were crammed onto a wagon serving as a stage at the dance floor's edge.

Beside Nettie, her sister, Stella Clayton O'Neill, tapped her foot, her red curls bouncing as her body swayed in time to the music. "I don't see why Finn had to play. There are plenty of other musicians."

Nettie's brother-in-law, his parents, and her parents played instruments for the dancers and listeners. She and her sister had been asked to dance almost every song and had moved to the side to rest their feet. Even Josh had twirled her around the floor two heavenly times.

Tables near the kitchen door held enough food to feed many times the number of people gathered. In the dark trees beyond the lanterns, fireflies blinked their courting ritual while a chorus of crickets chirped. Nettie swatted at a mosquito, an inevitable pest at any outdoor summer gathering.

Lance, her sixteen-year-old brother, had surprised her and asked Josh's fourteen-year-old sister, Rebecca, to dance several times. The two blonds looked more like brother and sister than friends. At least Lance had shot up in height since they'd been here and was a head taller than Rebecca.

Kathryn McClintock sat beside her and watched her oldest son. "I can't believe Josh is twenty-four. Seems only a few weeks ago we bought him his first pair of boots."

Nettie admired Kathryn, an attractive woman in her forties whose blonde hair was slightly darker than Nettie's. The other woman had been extremely kind to the Claytons since they'd moved to McClintock Falls. In addition, Kathryn knew a lot about healing and midwifery and helped many families in the community.

Kathryn gasped when Josh kissed a beautiful woman with dark hair. "Oh, I wish he wouldn't associate with Isobel Hamilton."

"She lives next door to us. I don't know her, though. She isn't out much in the daytime." Nettie slapped her hand over her mouth.

Her cheeks heated and she couldn't believe she'd been so awful. "I didn't intend to say that aloud."

Kathryn laughed, her blue eyes twinkling like those of her son. "But that's exactly my point. I'm the one who should be ashamed for gossiping, but I just don't trust that woman."

From her other side, Stella pursed her lips. "She's not our sort, Nettie, so there's no point trying to be her friend."

Nettie couldn't help staring at the woman Josh hugged to his side. The sight had Nettie battling knives of envy stabbing at her heart.

"I try to be friendly to everyone. Doesn't mean I have to be bosom pals."

Kathryn patted her arm. "Very commendable, dear."

In spite of her declaration to be friendly, Nettie resented the beautiful brunette. Men paraded to her door almost every night, or so it seemed. While she hadn't seen Josh there, that didn't mean he hadn't been.

After all, Nettie tried to ignore what went on at the house next door. Still, she couldn't help her crush on the tall, dark Josh McClintock even though she knew her dreams were hopeless.

The band took a break and Papa and Mama came over with Lance and Finn following.

Papa said, "Time we went home, Nettie."

Mama took Kathryn's hand in both of hers. "Such a nice party. Thanks for inviting us."

Kathryn stood and hugged Mama. "Thank you for furnishing the music. I didn't intend that to happen when I invited you."

"We enjoy playing, which is why we brought our instruments." She shifted the mandolin to her other hand. "Well, I suppose we'll see you at church Sunday. Goodnight."

"Come again, anytime, but please make a visit soon." Kathryn waved.

Stella and Finn followed her and her family to the wagon. She and her lovely sister exchanged hugs.

Smiling at Finn, Stella said, "In spite of me complaining about Finn playing tonight, I'm happier than I ever dreamed I could be."

Finn pulled her to his side and glanced at her with brown eyes filled with devotion. "So am I, my love."

Would anyone ever look at her in that way? With a sigh of longing, Nettie climbed into the wagon and settled onto the bench Papa put in for her and Lance.

Going home without Stella still didn't seem right. Her sister had been married four months now. She and Finn had their own home on a ranch not far away. Although Nettie was pleased at Stella's happiness, she still missed seeing her sister each day. The two had always been best friends.

She waved goodbye to Stella and Finn. "I had such a nice time and danced so much, I'll sleep like a rock tonight."

Lance looked at her. "Huh, you always sleep like a rock. A tornado whirling through couldn't wake you."

"I can't help myself. I need my rest at night."

Why did people always comment on the fact she was such a sound sleeper? Good heavens, what difference did it make? Would her family prefer she lie awake half the night battling insomnia?

Mama reached back to pat her shoulder. "At least you're full of energy when you wake, dear."

Partially mollified, she said, "Thank you, Mama."

Once home, they quickly locked the door and climbed the stairs to their beds. Nettie loved her room with pink striped paper and little pink roses between the stripes that matched roses blooming on the trellis right outside her room. She raised the window and leaned out to inhale the fragrant blooms.

She was grateful her family had moved to McClintock Falls. The home they rented was close to town and still not far from her sister's ranch. Papa could easily walk to the barber shop he operated in town. Kathryn had found furniture for this house that was better than any they'd ever owned. Come fall, Nettie was scheduled as the teacher since last year's teacher married.

The only drawback to this arrangement was that the home stood next door to Isobel Hamilton. She suspected the beautiful woman of loose morals. Certainly, she possessed Josh McClintock's admiration. Oh, well, none of her business. Perhaps envy colored her opinion.

The Mitchell's on the other side were a lovely couple with four kids. Grandpa McClintock owned the house the Claytons rented, the nicest place they'd ever lived. She was thankful to be here, glad her parents had a more satisfying and easier life.

As she snuggled down in her bed, a gentle breeze carried the flowers' perfume into her room. Nettie not only loved this room but living in this community, too. Finally, she was truly happy. With a smile on her face, she drifted to sleep.

***

Josh's friends still hefted tankards of beer but he set his down with a clunk. "Fellas, got a date with Ishoh…Issshobelll. Promised ta give me muh birthday presst…presshent."

With difficulty, he mounted his horse, Spartan, and rode toward the widow's home. Eager to finish his birthday up close and personal with the seductive woman fulfilling her whispered promises, he fought to focus and clear his head.

Yeah, there was her house.

He left Spartan's reins trailing the ground, the horse's signal to remain where he was. When Josh tried the front door, he found it locked and chuckled. The little minx and her games. Staggering to the side, he looked up at her bedroom window. Dark, but he'd bet she was waiting on her bed wearing only a tempting smile.

She'd left the window open, an invitation or he missed his guess. He tossed his hat at the opening but missed and the Stetson landed on the ground behind him. No matter, he wouldn't need it tonight. Using the trellis as a ladder, he climbed up and crawled through the window. After unbuttoning his shirt as he walked toward the bed, he flung it at the window.

"Baby, mm herrre fur muh burfday presshent." Whew, the room spun and he fell across the bed.

***

Nettie awoke and lay listening to birds calling. After her lovely evening and sweet dreams that followed, she woke up looking forward to the new day. She tried to swing her feet to the floor but something heavy pressed on her legs.

Good Heavens, had she suffered a stroke while she slept? She opened her eyes and sat up. Oh, no, this was worse.

Much worse.

Josh McClintock lay sprawled across her bed wearing no shirt and pinning her legs. She poked him. He didn't move.

She shook his bare shoulder. "Wake up. Josh? Move. Off. Me."

He groaned but didn't wake.

Dawn's light pouring through her open window indicated the time must be near six o'clock. Papa and Mama would be awake any minute. The kitchen where Mama would prepare breakfast was right under this room.

Pushing on Josh, Nettie pried her legs out from under his body. She tugged her nightgown free, thankfully without tearing it. Propping her knee against the mattress, she pulled his legs. When his feet hit the floor, she thought surely he'd awaken. But he didn't. Ha, and people thought she slept soundly.

How could one man be so heavy?

Grabbing his shoulders, she tugged him toward the edge of the bed. "Come on, wake up and go back out the window before anyone sees you."

He flung out his arms at her without opening his eyes. "Baby, where's muh present?"

Evading his groping hands, she slapped at his arms. "Not here, I guarantee you."

When that got no response, she pounded on his back. "Wake up, you crazy drunk."

A rap sounded at her door. "Nettie? What's Josh's horse doing in front of our house?"

Good Heavens, who else had seen his familiar horse? Papa seeing the animal was enough. "You'd have to ask him."

Giving up on getting Josh to awaken and climb out the window, she tugged him to the floor. He hit with a loud thump. Except for the noise, she thought it served him right.

"Nettie? Why haven't you opened the door?"

"Just a minute." Bracing her back against the wall for leverage, she pushed Josh under her bed. Hurriedly, she climbed back between the sheets. To hide Josh from anyone standing in the doorway, she draped her quilt to the floor on that side of the bed.

The knob turned and Papa came inside, followed by Mama.

"Good morning." She brushed her hands across her face and shoved away hair that had escaped her braid.

Papa strode over to the window. Oh, no, she hadn't noticed the shirt Josh had left hanging half in and half out on the sill.

Her father snatched the garment and narrowed his eyes. "Explain Josh's shirt being here."

She shrugged. "I guess he tossed it."

"And did he also toss his legs that are sticking out from the foot of your bed, young woman?" He walked over and kicked something, Josh's boots she supposed.

"Hey!" The mattress lifted as Josh tried to sit up. "Ow. Ow."

Papa jerked the quilt off the bed and tossed it aside.

"Come out from there like a man, Josh McClintock, instead of hiding under my daughter's bed. How dare you defile Nettie."

Her face hot with embarrassment, Nettie pulled the sheet up to her chin. "Papa, nothing happened here. He was passed out drunk across the foot of the bed when I opened my eyes. You know how soundly I sleep. I had no idea he was here until a few minutes before you came in."

Josh slithered out and staggered to his feet holding his head. He worked his mouth as if he needed a drink, which in her opinion was the last thing he was getting. After sitting on the mattress, he put a hand on each side of his forehead.

He peered at her father and frowned. "How'd I get here? What's going on?"

Papa stood with hands on his hips. "That's what I'd like to know. I get up to find your horse in our front yard. Then Mr. Mitchell points out your hat at the corner of the house. When I picked it up, Mitchell and I see your shirt hanging out Nettie's window like a flag on Independence Day. Explain yourself."

Her father's voice held a note she'd never heard. Outside, the birds stopped singing and flew elsewhere. Nettie wished she could fly away with them.

More alarm shot through her. "Mr. Mitchell? His brother is head of the school board." She'd lose her job before she even started. The enormity of this terrible situation hit her as if she were straw in a tornado.

Josh blinked as if trying to focus. "Don't know how I got here. Musta got the wrong house."

Nettie hit his shoulder. "That's an understatement, Josh McClintock. How dare you climb in my window while I'm asleep. Now I'll likely lose my teaching position because of your drunken stupidity."

Papa looked from one to the other of them. "This is serious. Nettie's reputation will be ruined. And the school board will fire her before she even has a chance to start teaching. No one will believe she's innocent."

Papa looked at her and she wanted to shrink from the coldness in his eyes. "Young woman, you get dressed." He handed Josh his shirt. "Come downstairs with me while you put this on."

As they walked away, Josh said, "Honest, sir, I'm pretty sure nothing happened."

"Pretty sure? That's not good enough, Josh. You can imagine what our neighbors think. What will anyone who passed by this house think? Gossip spreads like wildfire. What do you think this will do to Nettie's reputation?"

Mama stayed in the room. "Get dressed, young lady. You can't have a young man in your bedroom at night and expect nothing to come of it. This will have consequences."

Tears sprang to her eyes. "But this wasn't my fault. Nothing happened. I promise, Mama."

Her mother shook her head slowly and tossed her dark auburn braid over her shoulder. "You heard your father, Nettie. If what you said is true, being good is not enough. You have to present a sterling reputation to everyone."

"I'll go talk to the Mitchells and explain."

Mama shook her head slowly. "Won't help, dear. Last night Nancy Mitchell mentioned to me how happy you looked dancing with Josh. She will never believe you didn't fall for his charm and invite him here. Get dressed now and we'll go downstairs."

Within ten minutes, she was dressed and sitting on the parlor's sofa. Josh was sitting by the fireplace. Instead of his usual charming, dimpled grin, he looked poleaxed. Papa was in the other armchair, his fingers drumming on the armrest and a stern expression set on his usually smiling face.

She tried pleading her case once more. "Papa, what are you doing? I told you nothing happened. Why don't you believe me?"

Josh said nothing, just appeared as miserable as she was. Maybe more since she wasn't recovering from a hangover. Hands still on his head, he rested his elbows on his knees.

Her father leaned back, his shoulders slumped. "Lance has gone for Josh's parents. When they arrive, we'll discuss this further. Until then, Nettie, you help your mother prepare a large breakfast. I suspect Josh needs coffee."

"Yeah, and I need my dad to reason with you and fix this."

Raking his fingers through his blond hair, Papa glared at Josh. "I suspect you'll be surprised at your father's reaction."

She needed coffee too. More, she needed a way to extricate herself from what she feared would be an even more horrid situation. Escaping to the kitchen, she fought tears.

Mama was cutting out biscuit dough, dipping the shape in warm grease, and then laying it on the cooking pan. "We'll prepare enough for the McClintocks, including Daniel and Rebecca in case they come with their parents."

"You have to help me. Please, Mama. Don't let Papa continue with this."

Mama sent her a sad smile. "I'm sorry, dear. Some things have only one solution. You let your father take care of this situation. He really does know what's best."

Nettie wiped tears from her face. "Not if his idea involves forcing Josh to marry me. What kind of marriage would that be?"

Ignoring her protests, her mother cut thick slices of ham and placed them in the skillet. "Set the jam and butter on the table and then count out the plates and cutlery. I hope we have enough dishes and mugs."

By the time breakfast was ready to serve, Kathryn and Austin McClintock had arrived. A somber group sat at the table. Lance, Daniel, and Rebecca prepared their plates and mugs of coffee, and then excused themselves. Nettie saw them head for the covered front porch where there was a swing and a couple of chairs. How she wished she could escape with them.

"Eat, Nettie." Papa passed her the scrambled eggs.

She dumped a spoonful onto her plate. How could he expect her to eat when her life hung in the balance? Nevertheless, she took a biscuit and a small piece of ham.

Austin nudged his son. "Get some coffee down and eat what you can. You need to be wide awake for this discussion."

Josh glared at his father. "Discussion? Don't you mean sentencing? I thought you'd support me but looks like you and Mr. Clayton have already decided everything."

"I've always supported you when you were right, son." His father pointed a forefinger at him. "Neither Council Clayton nor I was so drunk as to climb in the window of an innocent young woman after leaving his horse in front all night and compromising her reputation."

Josh sipped his coffee and set down the mug. "Look, I said all I did was pass out. She never knew I was there until this morning. All that happened was I saw her nightgown and she saw me without a shirt on. Her gown was buttoned up tight so nothing showed."

Austin set down his fork on the plate. "Son, that's not all that happened. No telling how many people rode by here early this morning and saw your horse. Your hat's still lying on the grass. Council said your shirt was fluttering from Nettie's window. I've taught you that a man's responsible for the consequences of his actions."

Josh looked at Nettie's father. "I suppose you're going to use your shotgun and force Nettie and me to wed."

Papa met Josh's gaze. "I don't own a gun, Josh. I'm asking you as one gentleman to another."

Austin pointed his fork at his son. "I own a shotgun and I'll use it if necessary."

Josh leaned back and stared at his father. "Pa? You wouldn't shoot your own son."

Austin dug into his breakfast. "Don't push your luck, Josh. Your behavior has put me in a foul mood. I'm sorely tempted to knock you upside the head as it is."

Nettie wanted to disappear. Anywhere would be better than this humiliation. Marry a man who so obviously didn't want her? No matter that she'd dreamed of him, she definitely didn't have a forced marriage in mind. She used her napkin to blot tears from her face.

Austin stood and looked at those assembled around the table. "I'll arrange for the preacher to be here about four if you're in agreement."

After glancing at Mama for approval, Kathryn nodded. "I believe we can have everything ready by then. Rebecca and I will rush home to fetch our clothes for the ceremony and return to help Grace with the preparations."

She turned to Mama. "We'll bring food, too, for we have a great deal left from last night's party."

Austin went to the front door and called Daniel. "Take

your brother's horse and go to Dallas's. Tell him and Cenora to come at four for a wedding. Then, go to Stella and Finn's with the same invitation."

Mama called, "Stella may want to come before then to help her sister."

So, the wedding was arranged without input from her or Josh. She recalled how exciting she'd found organizing her sister's wedding a few months ago. Stella and Finn had been elated. Now, Josh appeared ready for an executioner and she was in tears. This was not at all the day she'd dreamed for her marriage.

Chapter Two

Josh dunked under the pump. Three cups of coffee had helped de-fuzz his brain, but then sent him to the privy. Cold water sluicing over his head and shoulders did little to improve his spirits, but at least his wits revived. What a dang rotten thing to happen. A great birthday followed by disaster.

Sure, he'd planned to marry someday, but not for five or six years. Being single with so many willing females was too much fun to shackle himself yet. Not that Nettie Clayton was ugly or waspish, but he couldn't imagine himself with the shy, proper woman.

Hell, she'd probably faint if she saw him naked. Or if he saw her. He couldn't imagine making love to her.

That last was a lie, for she was a beautiful woman with curves enough to tempt any man. He just couldn't imagine schoolmarm Nettie in the throes of passion. She'd probably lie stiff as a board with her eyes closed tight while he did all the loving.

Daniel handed him a towel. "Better hurry. Pa's waiting inside the Claytons' house but he's been to the door twice."

His anger boiled up and overflowed. "Let them all wait. The wedding's not until four. Can't they at least give me some peace until then?"

His brother hooked his thumb in his waistband. "I don't think so, Josh. What were you thinking to get so drunk you couldn't tell one house from the other?"

He tossed the towel at his brother and reached for his shirt. "Intent on ending my celebration with Isobel."

"That pretty widow had you thinking with the wrong head. I hope your night was worth all this fuss."

"Hell, I don't remember much after I left home." He examined the back of his hand. "Climbed a trellis and have the scratches to prove it. Pretty sure I passed out before prissy Nettie even woke up."

He fastened his shirt and tucked it into his denims. "Now I'm expected to pay for sins I didn't commit."

Soon he'd be changing into his best—his only—suit for his execution, otherwise known as his wedding to Nettie Sue Clayton. His mother and sister had gone to bring whatever the hell they were furnishing for the ceremony. He was stuck here under guard.

Daniel stared at him, a frown's vee creasing his forehead. "Don't know why you're so set against this. Nettie's a real nice woman and pretty, too."

How could he explain the trapped sensation swamping him like one of the hurricanes he'd read about? "I have nothing personal against Nettie. She's one of the best looking women I've ever met and is real nice. You know my rule—I stay away from her kind because they expect marriage and I'm not interested."

Daniel stuffed his hands in his pants' pockets. "Big brother, you better get interested fast. Mama and Pa are both determined to see you wed to Nettie. Plus, her dad is positive that's the right thing to do. He doesn't look like a man to mess with, especially not where one of his children is concerned."

Josh raked his hand through his wet hair. "The thing is, I did *not* mess with his daughter. If Mitchell hadn't seen my horse, I think I could have talked my way out of this."

His brother clapped him on the shoulder. "Not this time. Afraid your legendary charm doesn't impress Mr. Clayton."

Mumbling curses under his breath, Josh went back into the house. Unless he missed his guess, Daniel was supposed to be his guard and caretaker. Imagine, setting his younger brother against him—as if he would run off and disappear, leaving his family, obligations, and all he knew. This was a sorry situation all around.

They went into the kitchen and he took a seat at the table where Pa and Mr. Clayton waited with coffee and the remaining biscuits from breakfast. His stomach rumbled and he looked away from the food. Damn, his gaze landed on Nettie.

She refused to meet his glance but her eyes were puffy and red from crying. If she didn't want this marriage either, then why did they have to go through with the dang ceremony? Wait—he'd been pretty sure she was sweet on him, so how come she'd been crying? Appeared to him she should be pleased as could be.

Pa pushed the biscuits at him. "Better have something to soak up all that coffee. Long time until the wedding supper."

"And then what? I don't have anywhere to take a wife. We supposed to stay in her room or mine?"

"For the time being, you can live in the little house we save for Dallas's grandfather. Now that he's seen the baby, John Tall Trees doesn't expect to return until this fall. Dallas and Cenora are over there getting it ready for you and *your bride*."

Josh grimaced at the verbal jab. He met his father's gaze. "You don't have to hammer at me. I said I'd marry Nettie so can we just move on?"

Nettie threw down the towel she'd used to dry dishes and hurried from the room. Mrs. Clayton rushed after her.

Rebecca stood with hands on her hips. "Now see what you've done? How can you be so mean when you talk about marrying Nettie?"

Josh split the biscuit and slapped a piece of ham between the two halves. He refused to make eye contact or speak to anyone until the dadgum wedding.

Nettie ran up to her room and threw herself across her bed. How could this be happening? All those nights she'd longed for a man like Josh seemed foolish. Who was she kidding? She'd yearned for Josh, dreamed of him suddenly falling desperately in love with her.

Not only were all her plans destroyed, the man she desired would be hers unwillingly. If he didn't want her, then she didn't need him. She certainly didn't cotton to a man who got so drunk he had no idea where he was. That he made it up the trellis without falling was a mystery.

How long she lay there she didn't know. Sounds drifted up from downstairs. Staying in her room might be cowardly, but she didn't care. These were her last few hours here in her lovely room.

She must have cried herself to sleep because rapping on

her door roused her.

Mama carried in her wedding dress. "We don't have much time. Put this on."

Heart aching, Nettie rose from the bed and dried her eyes. "This is the worst day of my life."

Mama laid the garment on the mattress with care before she turned to help Nettie. "Nonsense, dear. I know you don't believe it now, but this will all work out for the best. I feel deep in my soul that yours will be a happy and long union."

She allowed her mother to unfasten her calico dress. "How can you say that? How can I even face Josh knowing how he feels about marriage and me? My life is ruined."

"I can tell you're sweet on him. I also remember how he looked at you when we were in Lignite."

"He was flirting, Mama. That's what he does. It means nothing to him. Probably charms women as naturally as other men breathe."

"In time the two of you will settle and become a happily married couple. Now hold up your arms so I can slide this over your head."

Like an automaton, Nettie complied. No one seemed to care that her lifetime plans were destroyed. No one cared that Josh didn't want to marry her. No one cared, that is, except her. She admitted Josh's plans had also gone awry, but she had no sympathy for him. After all, he'd created this mess.

Nettie turned to gaze into the mirror. The gray silk that had looked stunning with Stella's dark red hair made Nettie appear pale and drab.

Mama tilted her head and appeared to assess Nettie. "We can use the pink roses for a bouquet and maybe in your hair."

"I look half dead. This color isn't good for me."

"You look lovely, dear. When we've arranged your hair, you'll look even more beautiful. I hope your sister arrives in time to help. She's so much better with hairstyles than I am."

Nettie turned first one way and then another. The silk glided over her skin as nothing she'd ever worn. The style was outdated but so exquisite she didn't mind.

Matching ruching ran around the bottom skirt's hem.

Three pointed panels formed the overskirt. Large tassels anchored three rosettes of gray satin and silk where each panel joined. Long sleeves fit closely beneath a puff at the upper arm near the shoulder. Small tassels decorated the base of the puff. Elegant gray lace rimmed the neck and tiny buttons marched down the front to a belt of gray satin.

"Mama, with all the hurry at Stella's wedding I never got to ask how my grandparents could afford such an elegant dress for your wedding? I remember they lived in a very plain small cottage. I always thought they hadn't much money."

"They were poor, but my mother's best friend worked in a fine manor. When your father and I became engaged, the good lady saved this clothing for me when her employer grew tired of wearing it and would have thrown it away. Can you imagine such waste?"

"No, but I'm glad you had this for your wedding. I'll bet you were a beautiful bride."

Her mother smiled wistfully. "I think I was but you'll be even more gorgeous, dear. I'm so pleased to see both my daughters wed in my dress. It holds such happy memories for me."

But it wouldn't for Nettie. "I'll be careful with it. Maybe Stella and Finn will have a girl who'll wear this someday."

Mama met her gaze. "I'd love that so much. Perhaps you and Josh will as well."

Nettie couldn't think about coming together with Josh. After imagining being in his arms for months, the reality frightened her. Having his arms around her and cradling her near was very different from him making love to her. Only it wouldn't be love, would it? No, he would be slaking his lust.

She knew where the expression "scared spitless" came from. Her mouth was dry as cotton. If only her eyes were that dry instead of tearing at the least mention of the wedding.

A knock preceded Stella hurrying in. She wore her new green dress to replace her favorite that had been ruined in an accident. "You look beautiful. Oh, except your eyes."

She snatched the towel from the washstand and poured water on the cloth. "Fold this and hold it on your eyes while I work on your hair."

Nettie allowed her sister to guide her to a chair and gave over to being pampered. "Mama suggested pink roses in my hair."

Mama peered out the window. "I'll get my shears and cut some flowers for a bouquet and your hair."

When she'd gone, Stella pulled Nettie's hair this way and then the other. "I was never so surprised as when Daniel told us about the wedding. You in any kind of trouble is the last thing I'd ever imagine."

Taking the cloth from her eyes for a second, Nettie jerked her head to stare at her older sister. "You think you were surprised? Imagine waking from a sound sleep to find a half-naked man lying across your legs."

Stella gently nudged her. "Put the cloth back on your eyes. I'll bet Papa was livid."

"I've never heard that tone in his voice and hope I never do again. I can't begin to tell you how upsetting this morning was."

Her sister held a strand of hair in one hand and brush in the other. "What did Josh say?"

"He has a hangover so powerful he can hardly hold up his head. Honestly, I don't understand why anyone would drink enough to give himself that kind of pain. He said he must have been confused and come to the wrong house. You know where he was going."

Stella tut-tutted. "Isobel Hamilton's, of course. She was all over him like fleas on a dog last night but she left about the time we did."

She shrugged. "Josh apparently kept drinking."

"He seems sober now. Didn't speak to me when I came in. Sat staring at the floor. Papa and Mr. McClintock still act angry with him."

"How do you think I feel? I had that nice teaching position all lined up. I love this house and my room here. Our family was happy and doing well. Papa has a safe indoor job with the barber shop. Things were perfect."

Her sister's voice was soft and sweet. "Now, Nettie, you know you've been sweet on Josh since he came to Lignite to help Finn. And you looked so perfect last night when you danced together."

"Humph. How I felt about him has changed since he climbed through my window and ruined my life. Besides, he thinks marriage is worse than prison."

Her sister held each side of Nettie's head. "For heaven's sake, be still. I just know you'll be the best wife ever. Josh will change his mind once he's been married to you for a little while."

Nettie tossed the blasted wet cloth onto the washstand. "You can't be sure of that. What you can be sure of is that he is only marrying me under duress. If, that is, he goes through with the ceremony." She'd be even more humiliated if Josh took off to who knew where.

Still, she had to ask her sister before Mama returned. "Does it hurt? I mean coming together with Finn."

"A twinge the first time but worth the momentary discomfort. He is such a considerate and gentle lover. I'm the luckiest woman alive. Oh, but I'm sure Josh will be as good because he's had so much practice."

Nettie met her sister's gaze in the mirror. "T-That's not as much comfort as I'd hoped you'd provide."

"Don't worry, Nettie. You'll be so surprised at how wonderful making love with your husband can be. I never dreamed until our wedding night."

"I see." But she didn't. Sure she knew the clinical explanation of what happened, but the actual event was a mystery.

Stella patted her head. "There, I think that looks perfect. All I need are the roses, but we'll wait until just before the ceremony to add them so they won't wilt."

Mama came back into the room looking pale and carrying a bucket of roses. "Twenty minutes until the ceremony. Preacher's here and so are Zarelda and Vincent McClintock."

Nettie definitely wanted to run away. "Oh, no, not Josh's grandmother. The woman never smiles and scares me speechless. Unlike Josh's mother, his grandmother disapproves of everything and everyone."

With a nod, her mother set down the roses. "She's already told Kathryn and me what we're doing wrong. That's after she lit into Josh. Dallas and Cenora got their share too. Apparently Rebecca is the only person she approves. Believe me, I was happy I had an excuse to rush up here."

Stella sorted through the flowers. "I'll use the buds. Oh, sister, you're so lovely. I can't imagine a prettier bride anywhere."

To appease her sister, Nettie merely said, "Thank you."

Remembering how Stella looked on her wedding day, Nettie knew she couldn't compare to her sister. Plus, Stella had radiated happiness. Finn had acted as if he'd been made king. What a difference in their wedding day and hers.

No more! She refused to accept this twist of fate lying down. Darned if she wouldn't start her marriage with a backbone. Josh McClintock had a few lessons coming his way.

Chapter Three

Nettie inhaled slowly, hoping she didn't lose her resolve. Gone was shy Nettie. From now on, she'd stand up for herself. Even Zarelda McClintock wouldn't intimidate her.

Papa waited for her at the bottom of the stairs. Beyond him, she saw the room filled with Josh's kin and hers. Even the Mitchells had been invited and their children sat on the floor in front of them.

As she stepped off the last tread, she took Papa's arm. Finn's mother played a violin and his father played the concertina. Odd choice for a wedding but the sound was pleasant.

Near the window, Josh stood with the minister. Wearing a dark suit, white shirt, fancy gray vest, and black western string tie, no man had ever been more handsome. Light from the front window cast light on his dark hair.

Raising her head, she fought to appear as if this were an ordinary wedding with her groom excited to win her hand. She wore a fine silk gown and Stella had created a lovely hairstyle with pink rosebuds woven among the curls. The small bouquet of roses and daisies in her ice-cold hands shook slightly. She'd never before appeared this well dressed.

Reverend Hopkins smiled at her. Such a kind man. She forced a…not really a heart-felt smile but as close as she could manage. Papa kissed her cheek before he handed her to Josh, who appeared surprisingly civil.

Nettie battled tears but kept her head high and her eyes dry. This was the only wedding she'd ever have and she intended to have everything about the day go smoothly. Reverend Hopkins opened his Bible and began.

Beside her, Josh acted as if he were frozen to the floor. What if he turned and ran out the door? Worry kept her from concentrating on the preacher's words.

Until he asked, "Do you have the ring?"

She panicked, but Josh pulled a ring from his vest and slid it onto her finger. Meeting her gaze, his blue eyes shone cold and his expression inscrutable. Perhaps he wanted to appear willing to those gathered, but she knew his true feelings. Probably everyone here did as well. This wedding was his fault and she had no reason to feel guilty.

She stared at the symbol of undying devotion and almost came undone.

Finally, the minister said, "You may kiss the bride."

Josh looked at her as if he expected her to run away. She offered her cheek, but he cupped her chin and kissed her right on the lips. Although he only brushed her lips, she almost dissolved into a puddle right there.

Reverend Hopkins closed the Bible. "Friends, I present Mr. and Mrs. Joshua Victor McClintock."

She and Josh turned to accept smiles and good wishes from friends and family.

Even Zarelda McClintock deigned to greet her. "About time this young scalawag settled down."

Josh accepted his grandmother's kiss but didn't reply to her jab. He seemed to have misplaced his charm today.

Papa raised his hands. "You're all invited to the wedding supper, most of which has been provided by Kathryn and Austin."

After everyone present had greeted her and Josh, they found a seat. From her point of view, the supper dragged on and on. In fact, the mantle clock showed only an hour passed before she felt she could escape.

Nettie leaned to speak to her new husband, "Excuse me, I'll go change out of this dress."

"You look real pretty, Nettie."

"T-Thank you. You look very handsome." She stood and headed for the stairs.

Josh watched his new wife ascend like royalty. He'd known she was pretty, but hadn't realized how beautiful. If he had to be married, at least his wife was a beauty and knew how to cook. He remembered the good vittles she'd made when he visited her family in Lignite before their move here.

Before the wedding, he'd lugged her trunk out to the

buggy. Now, he wanted to bang his head against the wall. Instead, he smiled as Grandpa clapped him on the back.

His grandfather hooked an arm across his shoulders. "Reckon that's the end of your carousing, son. Got yourself a real nice little wife there. Lucky for you she's quite a looker."

Josh sensed himself tense up even more, but he wouldn't disrespect Grandpa. "She's pretty all right."

Why did everyone harp on his so-called carousing? He was fed up hearing about his faults. Didn't all young men who had red blood in their veins have a few drinks and go out with pretty women? His friends sure as hell did.

In his opinion, he was taking on the yoke of marriage way too soon to suit him. Nettie was back downstairs dressed in the blue dress she usually wore to church.

He met her at the base of the banister. "You ready to leave?"

"Yes." She didn't meet his gaze.

He noticed her taut face so he reckoned she was as tired of this farce as he was. He gently guided her. "Then let's make our way to the buggy."

Amid cheers, catcalls, and good wishes, they rushed outside. He helped her up to the seat and jogged around to climb in. With a flick of the reins, and with his horse's reins secured behind them, they were on their way to their new, temporary, home.

As they drove away, she sighed and leaned back against the seat.

He tugged loose the bow on his tie. "Good to be out of there. I can hardly wait to get out of this suit."

She didn't answer.

"Well, Mrs. McClintock, are you eager to get to your new home?"

She sent him a curious glance then faced forward. "I'm curious to see what the house looks like. I expect the place is small since Dallas's grandfather lives there alone and for only a part of each year."

"Pretty nice place. John Tall Trees doesn't need much, but Pa and Dallas saw he had as fine a set up as John would allow. Imagine Dallas's grandfather will move here before long, especially now that Dallas and Cenora have a kid."

"I've never met an Indian. I know Dallas is half Cherokee, but I mean a full-blooded Indian in buckskins and such."

He laughed. "I'll remember to tell John to bring out his regalia."

She ignored his teasing and gazed around gloomily. She thought they must be near Cenora and Dallas' home. "Imagine, having a fully furnished house that's vacant most of the year. Must be nice to have McClintock resources."

"You know the saying. All a rancher or farmer wants is to own his land and the land that touches his."

She brought her fingers to her throat as if in alarm. "Oh, I apologize if that came out rude. I intended no offense. I know you and your family have worked hard for all you have. But many people work hard and never achieve success."

His response was a slight shrug of his shoulder. "Ours is mostly because Grandpa had the brains to stake out land and then the town. His father came in the 1820's with Stephen F. Austin's group of three hundred when Grandpa was a kid. My great-grandfather bought up a few land grants. Grandpa continued buying up land, a little here and there. By then there was a village called McClintock Falls, but Grandpa staked out a regular town and sold lots. Organized the citizens and made rules."

Rules. His family was big on the rules he hated. Sure he wanted to be a rancher, but he didn't have to do everything the same as everyone else, did he? Why couldn't he have lived his life the way he chose?

Now he was stuck. He supposed Nettie Sue wasn't that bad, if you liked the pure-as-the-driven-snow type. Which he didn't. He liked a woman who knew how to enjoy living and made life fun for those around her. Who could speak up for herself. Who had a backbone.

He exhaled his frustration. The one thing salvaging today's disaster was that at least he'd be making love to a pretty woman tonight. Wouldn't be bad having a curvy woman to cuddle up next to each night when he was through with work.

Of course with her warming his bed each night he'd be faithful, but that didn't mean he had to hang around with her all the time, did it? Hell, no. He'd be spending the same amount of time with his friends as before.

As they drew near, a light burned in the window of the cottage. Nice touch. He figured he could thank Cenora for that.

He reined in the horses and set the brake. "Here we are. You go on in and I'll lug in your trunks."

She stared at him. What was she thinking? Couldn't the woman he'd seen jumping out of her father's wagon get down from the buggy unassisted?

"Okay, wait there and I'll come around to help you." He hopped out and lifted her. After he lifted her by the waist, he made sure to slide her slowly down his front. Let her get used to being close to him.

She stepped away and straightened her skirt. "Thank you." Picking up a valise, she headed for the house.

As he brought things inside, she pointed.

"The large trunk is my hope chest and goes in here. The smaller one holds my clothes and goes in the bedroom." She turned and carried the valise into the bedroom.

She reappeared and studied the range. "I suppose I'd better lay the fire for in the morning. Looks like your mother sent some of the leftovers for us to have tomorrow. She's thoughtful."

She busied herself putting away all the folderol she'd brought. Other than a little food, they shouldn't need much. John Tall Trees lived here just fine. When she appeared satisfied with the kitchen and parlor, she stood as if surveying her progress.

He yawned and stretched. "Guess it's time to turn in."

"Yes, I'm tired. Goodnight." She hurried into the bedroom and closed the door.

Goodnight? He rapped on the bedroom door but it wouldn't open. "Open the door. You're my wife. We're supposed to sleep together."

"I'm not sleeping with you. I hardly know you. Do you think I'm deaf? I heard clearly enough you don't want to be married to me."

"But we're married just the same. Husbands have rights."

"Not unless they earn them. Don't think I don't know where you intended to go last night. I saw you at your party with Isobel Hamilton."

"Ha, you're jealous."

"Think what you want, but I don't want to sleep with a man and have him pretend I'm another woman."

"You mean one who's warm and inviting instead of cold and vengeful?"

"I mean one who shares her body with numerous men."

"Open the door and I'll show you what you've been missing. You'll be glad we're married then." He turned the knob but the door didn't open.

"Conceited, aren't you? Well, you see where your rowdy ways have landed you? Make yourself comfortable on the sofa."

"The sofa? After I helped your sister at her wedding. Didn't I help your folks move here and my folks found them a place to live and furniture? And then I went along with your father's edict today to save your reputation. Is this any way to repay me?"

"You also ruined my life. You can sleep on the sofa. Alone."

"Hell, I don't need a frigid woman anyway."

Her voice sounded smooth as honey but irritated him like stings from a nest of hornets. "Oh, I'm not frigid, dear husband. But you'll have to wait to find that out."

Josh kicked the trunk he'd moved to the side of the room then winced. Damn the woman anyway.

Inside the bedroom, Nettie was so angry she stomped to the bed. She couldn't explain how she could be crying and be furious at the same time, but she was. There was no armoire, so she hooked her best blue dress on a peg and opened her valise.

Someone, probably Stella, had exchanged her plain nightgown with the high-button neck for a beautiful lawn one with a rounded neck thin shoulder straps held together only by pink bows. The sight set her crying more and she tossed it aside. She'd sleep in her chemise.

She placed the nightgown in a drawer of the high dresser where she'd stored her clothes. Someone had already put Josh's things in the washstand drawers. Other than the bed and those two pieces of furniture, there was a table and a chair.

That barely left space to walk in the small bedroom. The dresser didn't match the other furniture, which looked to be handcrafted. The piece must have been moved in just for her and Josh. That thought made her sad.

She turned down the lamp and crawled into bed.

Alone.

On her wedding night.

Early the next morning, she readied for the day as quietly as she could. Easing open the door, she crept into the kitchen. Josh slept soundly, in spite of the fact he was far too long for the sofa. He'd left his britches on, but slept shirtless.

She couldn't help staring. His was a magnificent physique. Apparently ranch work built plenty of muscles. Like the other McClintock men, he was taller than most males she'd seen and handsome as sin.

With a sigh, she started the coffee, grateful the small cottage had a pump in the sink. When frying bacon created a tempting aroma, Josh woke. He stretched and pulled on his boots.

He rubbed his neck. "Sleep well, dear wife?"

She sent him her sweetest smile. "Perfectly, dear husband. Breakfast is almost ready."

He jerked on his shirt. "Uh, I'll be right back."

By the time he returned from the privy, she had the table set and loaded with food. She took her chair and flicked her napkin across her lap.

"Smells good." He reached for a biscuit.

She slapped his hand. "We should start as we mean to go on. You say grace."

"Me?" He stared at her as if she had two heads.

"You're head of the household."

He met her gaze, a chill in his blue eyes. "Could have fooled me last night." But he bowed his head and gave a short blessing.

She'd resolved to be friendly and a good wife as long as

he didn't go off drinking again. But they ate in silence. Needing to keep busy, she rose and cleared the table.

He remained seated, sipping more coffee while she did the dishes.

Drying her hands on a towel, she looked at him. "I suppose we'll be going to church today. If so, I'd better be getting ready."

"Wouldn't the head of the house decide that?" His jaw clenched with a slight tic.

She folded her hands in front of her. "What have you decided, Mr. McClintock?"

He exhaled and his face relaxed. "Might as well. Have to get through the day somehow. I'll need a clean shirt."

"I'll get you one." She walked toward the bedroom. Obviously he was no more comfortable alone with her than she was with him. That didn't cheer her.

He was up and beside her before she realized he'd risen. For a large man, he moved quickly and silently. "I can get my own shirt. Reckon it's in a drawer of the washstand."

"Y-Yes. Top drawer." Being in the small bedroom with him unnerved her. What if he seized the opportunity to repay her for locking him out last night and demanded his husbandly rights?

Shirt in hand, he paused and glared at her. As if he read her mind, he said, "Don't flatter yourself. I've never needed to force myself on a woman. There are plenty willing…even if my wife isn't one of them."

Realizing she worried her skirt into wrinkles, she forced her hands to her side. "Did I say otherwise?"

"Didn't need to. You looked like a scared rabbit with the wolf about to attack."

She straightened her shoulders and raised her chin. "I'm not a rabbit, although I suppose you do qualify as a charming wolf. Certainly the girls at your party couldn't resist your appeal."

He unbuttoned his soiled shirt and tossed it aside. "They were normal women, not prissy, uptight schoolmarms."

She pulled her gaze away from his powerful shoulders and broad chest. "I am not prissy, not uptight, and—thanks to you—not a schoolmarm." Thank goodness he pulled on the fresh shirt before she swooned.

"Don't keep throwing that up to me. I said I was sorry, didn't I. Lordy, how I'm sorry." Shoving his shirt into his pants, he reached for his razor. After pouring water into the bowl, he lathered his brush and smeared soap on his face.

Rather than snipe, she let the last insult slide. Mesmerized, she watched him shave.

He met her gaze in the mirror. "Haven't you ever seen a man shave?"

Shaking her head slowly, she took a step toward him. "Does it hurt?"

"Not unless I let the razor slip. Or don't lather up enough and my skin's too dry. Then it's like scraping the whiskers off with a jagged piece of glass."

She seized her brush. After unbraiding her hair, she groomed and swept the strands into a low bun that wouldn't be dislodged by her Sunday hat.

Should she be honest? Might as well. "I'm nervous about appearing in public for the first time since the wedding. I mean with our marriage being so sudden and all, there's bound to be unpleasant talk."

"Yep, they'll all think you're knock…are expecting." He stopped mid-stroke of the razor and stared at her. "Best not let on we slept in separate rooms last night."

A blush's heat swept over her face and neck. "I would never do such a thing."

He resumed shaving. "Just don't pay any mind to jokes at our expense. Men can be ribald and women catty."

Tilting her head, she watched the muscles of his broad back as he moved his arms. "I imagine a lot of young women will be heartbroken that you're no longer available."

"I expect you're right. No point pretending to be modest. You have any beaus lined up?"

"No hearts will be broken because I'm no longer available."

He tossed the towel beside the pitcher. "Thought Marvin Davis was sitting with you at the church social a couple of weeks ago." After brushing his hair, he donned his vest.

Amazing. His hair fell in place with one stroke. "I'm surprised you noticed. Marvin was simply being gentlemanly because he saw I sat with only my family for company."

"If you believe that, you're more naïve than I thought. He appeared more than a little eager to become better acquainted."

"You can't think he's interested in me romantically? I assure you he's just a friend." She bit her lip as she waited for his answer. Was Josh right? Marvin had been attentive.

He rolled his eyes. "You just proved I'm right." After pulling out his pocket watch, he said, "About time to leave. That what you're wearing?"

She looked down at her blue dress. "It's the best one I have. I can wear the pink one if you'd prefer." How embarrassing to have to admit she owned so few clothes. She grabbed her gloves and hat.

"You look fine. Just not used to having a woman get ready so quickly. Seems like Mama fusses for an hour before she's ready and so does Becky."

Relieved at his answer, she perched her hat in place and pulled on her gloves. "Your mother has a lot more to do and more people to take care of and feed. She sent our supper for last night and breakfast this morning. There's still some left for later today."

"I expect one of the families will invite us for Sunday dinner."

She picked up her purse then paused and faced him. "Oh dear, what if they both do?"

Rich, deep laughter rumbled from his throat. "First one asks gets us. Or, we can come back here and avoid having to put on a show for others."

"I don't really want to visit with either set of parents today. Talking to them yesterday was rather…unpleasant."

"You hit the nail on the head there. Well, let's just see what we're offered." He extended his arm. "Shall we go?"

Chapter Four

Every head turned their way when they arrived at church. Nettie wanted to disappear, but she held her head high and planted a smile on her face. There had to be a first time to appear in public as a married couple. They wouldn't escape speculation by delay.

Josh acted the gallant gentleman and she remembered to smile at him. She hoped she was a good enough actress to get through the day. How could she help seeing people whispering while looking in her direction? And she knew what they must be saying.

As if to prove her correct, Mrs. Whitaker came over. "Why, Nettie, how clever of you to catch the most eligible bachelor in the county. Won't you share your secret?"

"No secret, we just decided to marry. We wanted a quiet family ceremony, so we didn't invite anyone except relatives."

The woman would not let the subject rest. "Now, you must tell me all about your courtship."

Josh slid his arm around her waist. "Not much to tell, Mrs. Whitaker. I met Nettie when I went to check on Finn's injuries a while back. Just couldn't get her out of my mind. You'll excuse us, won't you? I need to speak to my cousin."

He steered her toward Dallas and Cenora. Nettie was so discomfited by the elderly gossip that she couldn't even tell him how grateful she was. Thank heavens Mrs. Whitaker didn't follow.

Dallas beamed at them. "Say, cuz. Didn't expect to see you today."

Nettie took Cenora's hand. "Thank you for loaning us a place to live and for getting the house ready. You're very kind."

"Sure and you're that welcome." Balancing baby Houston on her shoulder, Cenora leaned in to speak only for

Nettie. "You know, your wedding was not that different from ours, except Dallas was wounded saving me life. I know how awkward you must feel, though. Don't fash yourself, Nettie. Things will be all right."

Nettie fought tears. "Thank you for saying so, but I don't know. Josh resents me so much and, and now I've embarrassed my family. They'll never think of me in the same way again."

Taking a moment to move the baby and cradle him on her arm, Cenora linked her other arm with Nettie's. "Let's sit by one another inside and then you can come home with us for dinner."

"I'd love that but let me ask Josh."

Beside her, he chuckled. "I heard the invitation. Sounds great to me."

The four went into the church. Chatting with one another kept others at a distance. Thank heavens, no more cross examinations from another gossip like Mrs. Whitaker. At least, not until after church.

They'd just sat on a pew when a nice looking couple leaned in to speak to them.

The man had dark blond hair and kind brown eyes. He extended his hand to her. "Kurt Tomlinson and this is my wife, Dorcas. Came to congratulate Josh."

Josh stood and shook Kurt's hand. "Nice to see you both."

"Best wishes, Nettie. I'll look forward to getting to know you." Dorcas's sweet smile lighted sparkles in her soft brown eyes. She tugged at her husband's sleeve. "Reverend Hoskins is ready to start the service."

Cenora leaned near Nettie's ear. "Kurt used to be Josh's best friend. He and Dorcas are really nice people."

Nettie filed away that tidbit. Had she seen the Tomlinsons at Josh's party? She didn't think so and wondered why they hadn't attended.

As soon as the service was over, she pasted on a smile and let Josh hurry her to the buggy. Waving at those streaming out of the church, they set off toward Dallas and Cenora's home.

She leaned back against the tufted leather seat. "Word certainly traveled fast about our wedding. Makes me wonder if someone went door to door."

"Living in a small town offers no privacy." His face gave no clue to his thoughts.

"Thank you for accepting Cenora's invitation."

He sent her a puzzled glance before he focused on the road. "Why wouldn't I? Surely you know Dallas is like my big brother. He came to live with us when he was twelve and I was nine. I've always looked up to him."

She wondered if Josh had ever resented losing the designation as oldest boy in the household. If so, he didn't appear to harbor any ill will now. "I don't know them well, but they both seem very nice. Cenora is awfully pretty, isn't she?"

Josh chuckled. "Yeah, she's a beauty. Don't get on her bad side, though, or she'll slice into you with her tongue. Lady has a temper."

"I remember Finn told Lance he didn't want a wife with red hair and a temper because of Cenora. Isn't it funny that he fell in love with Stella who is so much like his sister?"

"You think so?" He raised his eyebrows. "Naw, they're nothing alike other than the hair. Maybe the temper. Very different women otherwise."

"I'm sure they are. The similarities I mentioned are obvious things you notice right away. Stella is a wonderful sister. I can always count on her."

"But she's educated somewhat. Cenora didn't even know how to read when she and Dallas married. He taught her and Finn and the O'Neills."

"Really? I'd be lost without books to read. Do you enjoy reading?"

"Some. I like Jules Verne and Mark Twain. Read Dickens. You?"

Hearing they enjoyed some of the same books excited her. Perhaps they had more in common than she'd believed. "My favorite is *Anna Karenina*, but I like Charles Dickens and Louisa May Alcott and Mark Twain and...oh, I just love to read."

"My parents have a lot of books for you to choose from

if you wish." He turned in at a tree-lined drive. "Ah, here we are."

He stopped the buggy in front of a two-story house painted soft yellow with green and white trim. Josh set the brake, hopped down, and came around for her. "I see Dallas in the barn unhitching their buggy. Looks like Cenora's gone into the house. I'll let you out then go water the horses."

She enjoyed having him lift her. He appeared to do so effortlessly. The way he slid her slowly down his body sent waves of heat through her but she pretended otherwise.

Straightening her skirts, she said, "Thank you. I'll go in and help Cenora with the food."

***

She had thought things were going well during the pleasant afternoon with Cenora and Dallas. As soon as they returned home, she busied herself thinking about what to prepare for supper. After the delicious meal shared with Cenora and Dallas, perhaps leftovers would do.

Josh came out of the bedroom tucking his shirt into his denims. He didn't meet her gaze. "I'm supposed to meet a couple of guys in town."

"Now? On Sunday?"

"Yeah, won't be long." He clapped his hat on his head and was out the door before she could protest.

How long was "not long"? After checking the things she'd unpacked last night, she picked up a novel and read. At eight, she cobbled together a plate of leftovers.

By nine, she had a hard time focusing on the book's words. Where was Josh? She couldn't help wondering if one of those "guys" he'd gone to meet was Isobel.

No matter how hard she fought, jealousy choked her as if a person grasped her throat. Silly to be envious when she knew Josh didn't care for her and never had, yet she couldn't push down her anger, hurt, and resentment. How inconsiderate to say he wouldn't be long and stay out for hours and hours.

Nettie readied for bed. She'd never lived in a cabin in the middle of nowhere. Uneasiness at the loneliness made sleep impossible. A little after midnight, she heard him stumble into the house. After tugging on her wrapper, she tied the belt.

She unleashed her fury, "So this is 'won't be long', is it? Married less than two days and you're off cavorting and drinking with your friends. Look at you, so drunk you can barely walk. It's a wonder you didn't choose the wrong house again."

He sat on the chair and removed his boots. "The last thing I need is a nagging wife."

"Nagging? Is it nagging to expect you to be courteous? Is it nagging to take you at your word?"

"Hell, yes, you're nagging. I didn't ask to be married. Don't think I'm giving up my friends and my life."

"You selfish man-child, all you're giving up is a drunken good time. I've lost my family's respect, my job, and ended up with a man I no longer even like and who doesn't like me. I promise you this, Josh McClintock, if you get drunk again, I'm locking you out." She turned and stomped to the bedroom and locked the door behind her.

After tossing and turning a couple of hours, she finally drifted to sleep. When she woke, Josh had already gone to work. She was miserable. Her first instinct was to rush to her parents' home, but she didn't want Mama to know how wretched she was.

Only a few days ago, she'd been so happy. She loved that her father was no longer risking his life and health in a coal mine. Her parents were living in the nicest house of their lives and she'd had a beautiful bedroom all to herself. With her salary, she could have helped her brother get a good education and fulfill his dreams to become a doctor.

The situation was enough to make her join the Ladies Temperance Union. No, she wasn't opposed to spirits, just to drunkenness. And here she was married to a man who equated getting drunk with a good time and being happy.

She'd vowed to be a good wife, so she wouldn't shirk her household duties. She cooked a pot of beans and had cornbread in the oven by the time Josh came in from work. He washed up without a word and sat on the sofa without looking at her.

After taking the cornbread out of the oven, she dished up bowls of the beans and set them, cornbread, butter, and honey on the table. She poured two mugs of coffee and put them by their food. Straightening her apron, she stood her tallest.

"Supper's ready."

"I'm hungry." He stood and came to the table.

"Will you say grace, please?"

He gave her such an aggravated glare she thought he'd refuse, but he bowed his head and mumbled a short blessing.

Searching for anything to break the ice, she asked, "What did you do today?"

He slathered butter onto his cornbread. "Worked on fence. Something or someone knocked down a long string of wire. Pa and I are betting a human culprit is responsible."

"You have any ideas who would do such a thing?"

Between bites, he said, "We have suspicions, but no proof. Pa bought up a ranch at a sheriff's sale just over a week ago. The man who lost the land held Pa responsible."

"But isn't a sheriff's sale when someone can't pay and is foreclosed on by the bank?"

"Yeah, but Tyson accused the banker's representative and the sheriff of conspiring to cheat him so Pa could steal the ranch. Place was so rundown no one can live there until repairs are made. Even so, Tyson's the sort who always thinks he's right and others are wrong."

"I hope you don't have more trouble with him. He wouldn't threaten to harm you and your father or Daniel, would he?"

He paused with his spoon halfway from the bowl. "Don't get your hopes up. You won't be a widow anytime soon."

"Josh, surely you know I only meant to offer concern for your safety and that of your family." How sad that he thought her capable of such meanness. She wanted to run to the bedroom and weep but refused to give into weakness. Darned if she wouldn't have a civil conversation with her husband.

Pensive expression on his handsome face, he reached for more cornbread. "Well, I don't know what Tyson is capable of, but we don't trust him. He's already broken the law by tearing out our fence line. We have some of our hands watching the water holes."

She couldn't hold back a gasp of surprise. "You think he'd poison your water and kill innocent animals for spite?"

"We're not taking chances. Don't think you're in any danger. He's crazy mean, but he's mad at Pa, not me or you."

"What about your family's home? I hope he wouldn't do anything there, either. Surely he wouldn't threaten Kathryn or Rebecca or Daniel to get back at Austin."

"We have a man watching there, too, and Mama knows how to use a gun. So do Daniel and Becky. If you don't, you need to learn."

"I've never shot a gun. Actually, I've never even held one."

"One day soon, we'll go out and you can learn. In the meantime, be careful. Like I said, I don't think you're in any danger, but there are always threats out here and you're always wise to be watchful." He pushed away from the table and walked back to the sofa where he picked up a book.

She cleaned the kitchen and washed and put away the dishes. "I'm going to bed. Goodnight, Josh."

Without looking up, he said, "Yeah."

Wishing for a graceful way to compromise, she was at a loss. What a messed up marriage.

The rest of the week passed in the same manner. No matter how civil she acted, Josh was surly and unresponsive. She knew he was as miserable as she was, but at least she made an effort to be a good companion.

How was she going to win over her husband?

Chapter Five

On Thursday, Josh rode to work with a full stomach and a bad attitude. He hated his life, his marriage, and feeling trapped. He hadn't asked to be married, had he? Hell, no. He could have explained everything to Mitchell and stayed a free man. Instead, here he was shackled to a woman impossible to please.

Damned if he wouldn't go out and have a little fun after work today. That cheered him up. He rode to the ranch singing a bawdy tune. Waving at Mama as he passed the house, he joined Pa and Daniel at the barn.

A few cottony clouds floated in the bright blue sky. The soft southwesterly breeze cooled the sun's rays. In the distance, a hawk floated high with wings outspread. This was the life he loved, the life he'd been born to, the life he planned to follow for as long as he lived.

Daniel drove the wagon holding cedar posts, barbed wire, and the tools they'd need to replace any fence they found down today. The family dogs, Brownie and Blackie, rode in the back. They traveled along the fence line that separated their land from that purchased at the sheriff's sale last week.

Josh gestured ahead. "Either Bob Tyson or someone else was busy overnight."

Pa shaded his eyes with his hand. "Damn the man. Must be at least a quarter mile section pulled over, posts and all."

"What are we gonna do about that man, Pa?"

Pa shook his head as if dismayed. "Damned if I know. We can't tolerate this any longer but I don't want an all-out war with Tyson. Losing his land is bound to be tough even though he did mismanage the place. I'm notifying Sheriff Yates. You boys start repairs and I'll be back as soon as I can." He turned his horse and galloped toward town.

Josh asked Daniel, "Hands watching the water holes report anything?"

His brother climbed down from the wagon. "Marcus thought he saw someone but when he called out, whoever it was disappeared. He didn't leave the water hole and give chase for fear the person would sneak in behind him."

"Probably would have. Doesn't take long to dump in poison."

Brownie and Blackie raced back and forth looking for rabbits or whatever the heck dogs searched for.

Daniel picked up a coil of rope. "You think we can pull the fence back upright and tamp in the posts?"

Josh assessed the problem. "Let's give it a try. Sure easier than stringing new fence."

By the time their father returned from town, the fence was up, all the posts tapped in, and wire tightened.

Pa rode up to them. "Looks good, boys. Yates said he'll talk to Tyson. Don't know what good will come of it. At least we've filed a complaint and the sheriff knows what's happening."

They rode checking fence until near suppertime. "You boys knock off for the day. I have to ride over and have a word with the men in the south pasture."

Daniel and Josh didn't argue. Giving his signal, Daniel sent both dogs back into the wagon bed. With a wave at his brother, Josh galloped toward town. He knew he was being ornery, but he didn't like a woman trying to run his life. Danged if he wouldn't show her who was boss.

Six hours later, he hummed to himself as he rode into the small barn behind the house. After he'd cared for his horse, he went to the door. It didn't open. He went to the front, but it was locked too.

He knocked and called, "Nettie, let me in."

"No. I told you if you went off drinking again I'd lock you out. You didn't let much time pass before you had to test me, did you?"

He banged on the door. "Let me in right now. A wife can't lock her husband out of his own home."

"I'm not the one who climbed through your window half naked and ruined your life. Your partying is the very reason we're in this mess of a marriage to start with. You sure don't learn easily."

"You're being vindictive for no reason. A man has a right to a night out once in a while with his friends."

"First of all, your so-called friends aren't very good pals if they let you get so drunk you don't know where you are. And they did. Now I've lost my job and any chance I had to help my family."

"Will you stop with that? I can help your family. I'm a successful rancher."

"Wrong. Your *father* is a successful rancher. You are no better than a hired hand. And you're acting like a spoiled little boy."

"That's a spiteful thing to say."

"Do you deny it? Do you deny you went to see that Isobel Hamilton?"

"Why do you think that?" He went to the window. Wouldn't budge. He peered through the glass.

Nettie was there, wearing her blue robe that matched her eyes and with her blond braid hanging down her shoulder. "All the windows are locked. If you want somewhere to sleep, little boy, go home to your mommy and daddy."

He turned away. "I hope you smother in there with no air coming in."

Wondering what the hell had happened to his life, he peered around the covered porch. He sure didn't want his parents to know he'd been drinking in the middle of the week. He might be grown but Pa wouldn't hesitate to clip him on the jaw. At least, that's what he thought Pa might do.

Using his hat to cover his head, he stretched out on the porch. Damn, he swatted at a mosquito on his neck. Thus ended a perfect evening in a perfect marriage.

The next thing he knew, the sun was up and he was drenched. Fighting awake, he sat up. Nettie stood in the doorway holding a dishpan.

He pulled his wet shirt away from his body. "You had no call to do that."

"Though it might help your headache and I wanted to wake you for breakfast, dear husband. You need a hearty meal before you go to work."

"That wasn't necessary. And I didn't go see Isobel. We might have married against our will, but I take the 'forsaking all others' to heart."

A surprised then soft expression came over her face. "I see. Coffee's ready. You have time to wash up and change shirts before the biscuits are done."

He accepted the enameled cup of coffee she poured him and carried it to the bedroom to shave and change. Shrew she might be, but she was one fine cook. He had to admit she was also a pretty sight to have in his home.

Ha, his home. This was her home and he was only here by her tolerance. He'd think of some way to reclaim his rights as head of household or his name wasn't Joshua Victor McClintock.

After breakfast, he rode to work on his family's ranch. Hired hand? Danged if that didn't go against the grain.

Pa stepped off the porch as he rode up. "Hello, son. How're you feeling? You're looking a little rough."

He dismounted and they walked toward the barn with him leading Spartan by the reins. "What do you expect when I'm married to a waspish woman?"

Dad shook his head slowly. "Son, you got to realize your actions ruined Nettie's plans."

"Didn't do mine any good either. Everyone seems to have forgotten that."

"No one's forgotten anything. For some time, your mother and I have been worried you were way too wild. Seems like you completely forgot our training. That's what landed you married to a woman you barely know."

A sledge hammer to his gut couldn't have had more impact. "You and Mama talked about me? About being worried about me?"

"On many occasions. Seems like you changed to a different set of friends and got more and more irresponsible."

Reeling from the discovery, he defended himself. "I do my work, Pa. You can't say I slight the ranch."

"I know you work hard here. I mean apart from this place. Seems to us you've been on a path to destruction."

His father stopped and held Josh's gaze. "Son, your

mother and I have worked hard to build this ranch into a major business. A lot of people depend on us for their livelihood. We worried about passing it on to you and our hard work going the way of Tyson's."

Now Pa had riled him to the core. "You think I care so little for this land?" He gave a broad, sweeping gesture. "Do you think I'd risk losing all this?"

"Not willingly. But what worries us most is the path your personal life has been on. I don't know what's changed, Josh, but something sure as hell has."

"Naw, you're imagining things, Pa. I just wanted to sow my wild oats. Now I'm married, I'll settle down."

"That's what your mother and I hoped. We like Nettie and you two appear well-suited. We put a lot of store in this marriage, son."

"Sure. Pa. I know you do. She's a pretty woman and a real good cook."

"Give her a chance, Josh. She has a lot to offer as a wife. She'll stand by you through thick or thin. Now, let's get the cattle moved to the new pasture."

All day his father's words kept rerunning in his head. He'd had no idea his parents had worried about him. Sure, he knew they wanted him and Daniel and Dallas to succeed and be happy, but he figured that was as far as it went.

Eating dust from the herd, he wondered how they could think he'd go crazy and lose his share of the ranch? This land was his life's blood. He laughed and looked down at his clothes. Right now he was wearing a good bit of his land.

Time passing did not reduce the shock of his father's revelation. He was still shaken to his boots. Mama and Pa thought he'd lost his way. Lost his mind.

That's what they meant. Didn't he go to church with them every Sunday? Sure he did. Well, almost every Sunday.

Except, he started counting up the times he'd missed this past year or two due to a hangover. More than he wanted to remember. More than he could count.

Had he changed friends? Well, maybe a few of his old friends didn't come around anymore. Maybe three or four of his best friends now were guys he'd only been chummy with the last year or two.

He reined in Spartan and watched the cattle move by. Well, hell. No wonder his parents worried about him.

Daniel shut the gate behind the last straggler. "Yahoo! Quittin' time."

"I couldn't have said it better myself, little brother. Time to go chow down." With a wave, he urged Spartan into a gallop.

Chapter Six

Nettie decided the morning was a good time for cleaning. Wearing her oldest dress and largest apron, she'd tied up her hair in a rag when she heard wagon wheels and a horse. She wasn't expecting anyone. She whipped off the head wrap and apron and hurriedly touched up her appearance.

Taking a deep breath, she opened the door and found her sister alighting from a buggy. "Stella, what a nice surprise."

Stella glided in wearing her best green dress. "I hope I'm not too early for a call and also that I don't need an invitation to visit. I brought us cake left from last night's supper."

She pressed her hands down her old tan dress, feeling dowdy in comparison to her attractive sister. "I was just cleaning, but I'll make us some tea."

Following her, Stella took a seat at the table. "Finn and I wanted you to come home with us on Sunday, but you left with Dallas and Cenora before we could ask."

"You know Josh and Dallas are like brothers. Cenora and Dallas cleaned up this cottage and put in a couple of extra pieces of furniture. I wanted a chance to thank them."

"You should ask them to eat with you and Josh soon."

"I will."

How lovely to have her sister here even if she was ordering her around. She'd been so lonely all day with no one else around. And uneasy at night when Josh wasn't here.

"We had a nice afternoon. They have an amazing house and ranch."

Stella's eyes widened. "Surely not as nice as Austin and Kathryn's? Theirs is like a palace in a rustic, folksy way. I've never been anyplace so lovely."

"Different, but as gorgeous. Of course, a lot of their furniture is handed down and given them by various family members. Except in their bedroom. Grandpa McClintock bought the entire room's pieces as a housewarming present when Dallas bought the ranch several years ago."

"How are you settling in to married life?"

"All right, I suppose."

Stella leaned forward, her eyes sparkling with mischief. "Tell me, is Josh as charming in bed as on the dance floor? Did he like the nightgown I slipped into your bag instead of that high necked kind you always wore?"

Nettie looked away. "Uh…well…you see, we haven't exactly, you know, yet?" She couldn't resist glancing to gauge her sister's reaction.

Eyes wide, Stella stared at her as if she's just said she worked in a circus. "What? You've been married almost a week. What's wrong?"

She pulled her handkerchief from her sleeve and dabbed at tears flowing down her cheeks. "W-We had a fight. Actually, more than one." She extended her hand. "Please don't tell anyone."

Stella covered Nettie's fingers with her own. "Of course not. I know you were upset you had to get married so suddenly, Nettie, but you've had a crush on him since we were in Lignite. What caused the fight?"

She withdrew her hand from the comfort of her sister's. "Different things."

"What kinds of things?"

"To start with, after the way he talked about marrying me, I was hurt and angry. I vowed not to be so shy and easily overlooked."

She stood and paced the small room, her anger at the situation returning. "Besides, I was so mad at him for causing the hasty wedding when I knew he'd intended to visit that awful Isobel Hamilton."

She turned and threw her hands wide. "Then, the very next night when we returned from visiting Dallas and Cenora, he went right out and got drunk and missed supper."

"Oh, no, the very day after your wedding. And on Sunday?"

She dropped onto her chair and blew her nose. "I told him if he did that again I was locking him out of the house. He said he didn't need a nagging wife."

"Evidently, he needs his rear kicked."

"As if to test me, last night he did the same thing. I'd warned him so I had to carry out my promise. So, I…I locked him outside."

Stella gaped at her. "You didn't? Outside his own home? What did he do then? Break down the door?"

She shook her head. "Slept on the porch. I woke him this morning by pouring a dishpan of water on him."

Crossing her arms on the table, she laid her head on them. "Oh, Stella, I'm so miserable." Between sobs, she moaned, "My life is ru-hoo-rrined and I d-d-don't know how to f-f-f-fix things."

"You poor dear." Her sister came around and hugged her, then moved her chair next to Nettie's. "First off, you have to end the arguing. You'll drive him into Isobel's or some other woman's arms. You know he could take his pick."

She sniffed and nodded. "I know, but he says he's been faithful."

"Oh, Nettie, you didn't accuse him of adultery?"

She tilted her head into a slow shrug. "Not exactly, but I might have insinuated. He said no matter what he thinks of marriage, he takes his vow of 'forsaking all others' seriously."

"Wonderful, that's half the battle won right there." Stella squeezed her hand. "Nettie, you have to make the first move. You've humiliated Josh by locking him out of his home and bedroom."

"Once…once I started, I didn't know how to change course. He can be easily as infuriating as he is charming."

Stella offered a stern shake of the head. "Don't assign blame, sister. You have to take the lead here."

She wiped at her eyes. "But how? I don't even know how to start."

"What are you making for supper?"

"Mama sent over a plucked chicken. I thought I might fry it."

"No, sister, roast it in the oven. And I'll tell you what else to do."

***

Nettie smoothed her curls over her shoulders as Stella had suggested. Nettie's pink dress was pressed and over it she wore a fresh apron. Worrying over the state of her marriage, she'd taken special care with her appearance, the meal, and made a peach pie for dessert.

Josh had told her they worked from "can 'til can't" so she didn't expect him until dusk. When she heard him ride up to the barn, she set the table. As soon as he came inside, she'd pour the coffee and invite him to be seated. For now, she waited expectantly beside the cupboard. The sound of his boots on the back steps set her in motion.

The kitchen door opened and Josh strode in. He stopped abruptly and sniffed the air. "Do I smell pie?"

"Peach. But first there's roast chicken with potatoes and fresh peas from Mr. Tall Trees' garden." The same place she'd found the flowers she cut for the table.

She picked up his cup. "Coffee's ready and I was about to take our dinner from the oven."

He assessed her. "You been to town, Mrs. McClintock?"

Shaking her head, she set their dinner on the table. No need to tell him about Stella's visit. At least, not yet.

"I've been here all day. Sewed some. Baked bread. The usual chores."

Seating herself, she waited for grace then served his plate. "How was your day, husband?"

He speared a piece of chicken with his fork. "Not that great. Another fence pulled down."

"That's terrible. Have you seen this man Tyson on McClintock land?"

Josh shook his head and ate as if he'd been starving. "Has to be him. Tyson had a real good place, too. Used to be a good moneymaker."

"What happened to change his situation?"

An odd expression came over Josh's face and he wouldn't meet her eyes. "Drinking, women, and gambling."

"Each of those surely can be a curse." She wondered if he recognized he'd been on the same road. From his expression, she thought he might.

"Surprised he didn't lose the ranch, but he lost everything else. Wife and kids left him. He'd let the place go to hell when the sheriff had to force him off the land. Owed back taxes and mortgage payments."

"That's sad. Must have amounted to quite a debt. Are the buildings usable?"

"Need a lot of work. Pa and I thought we might go over tomorrow and see what can be salvaged. Used to be a nice house and strong barns."

He pushed back from the table.

She refilled his cup. "You ready for pie?"

With a smile reminiscent of his old self, he rubbed his hands together. "Always."

After supper, he picked up his book and sat on the sofa. She cleaned up the kitchen and dried her hands. Gathering her courage, she sat beside him.

With a perplexed expression, he scrutinized her.

Praying for the right words, she composed herself. "Josh, I've been doing a lot of thinking. We should talk about our marriage."

He closed the book and laid it aside before he angled to face her. "I'm listening."

She'd practiced the words all afternoon, but now they were harder than rocks to spit out. "I hate the way things have been between us. Neither of us wanted to be wed, but we are. I think we should make the best of our situation."

He rubbed a hand across his jaw, his gaze never leaving hers. "What did you have in mind?"

"We should be courteous to one another. You know, you could be home when you say and not go off drinking any more. In return, I could be a better wife."

His blue eyes searched hers. "You offering to let me share your bed, wife? Have a real marriage?"

She looked at her hands. "I-I guess I am. If you're willing."

He cupped her chin so her gaze met his. "I'm willing. You know what that involves?"

"In theory." Thank heavens Stella had briefed her. Otherwise, she'd probably have made a bigger fool of herself.

Still appearing perplexed, he nodded. "That's good. Why don't you go get ready for bed? I'll be there in a few minutes after you've had some privacy."

"Thank you." What was she thanking him for? She was the one who'd made concessions.

"Nettie?"

She turned back. "Yes?"

"Leave your hair down. Um, please."

She'd no wish for another argument, so she scurried to the bedroom like the shy mouse she'd been most of her life. Drat, she'd found the courage to compromise. Darned if she wouldn't see this wedding night through without becoming a shrinking violet.

Quickly, she donned her fancy nightgown. My word, she could see right through the fabric. Plucking her courage, she ignored her image in the mirror and brushed her hair. After dabbing toilet water where Stella had told her, she lowered the light and climbed between the covers. She lay there shivering with trepidation.

You can *do* this. *You* can do this. You *can* do this.

He rapped. "You ready for me to come in?"

I'm not ready. I'm not ready. I'm not ready.

You can do this.

"Yes, I-I'm waiting in bed."

He opened the door, but the light was so low he appeared in shadow. He sat on his side of the bed and removed his boots. Then he took off his clothes. Oh, my word, all of them.

Instead of crawling in beside her, he turned up the lamp. "I want to see you. All of you."

"A-All? Of course he did. Stella had said he would, but she'd hoped Josh would be an exception and want to come together in the dark.

He lay down beside her and balanced on an elbow. "Don't worry, Nettie. We're married and this is what couples do. I'll try not to hurt or embarrass you."

His hand went to the ties of her gown. "Nice. Not like you wore at your parents' home."

"Not even mine. Stella sneaked this one into my valise

when she helped me pack."

A broad smile split his face. "I'll have to find a way to thank her." With a flick of each wrist he untied the pink ribbons that held up the fanciful creation.

When the garment would have dropped away, she gripped the edges to hold it over her breasts.

Gently, he removed her arms. "You're a beautiful woman and I'm your husband. You shouldn't be embarrassed for me to see you."

She gazed at him suspiciously. "Are you sure this is what other married couples do? From talk I'd heard in Lignite, I-I thought I'd just raise my gown and you'd, you know."

He shook his head slowly and offered a wry grin. "Where would be the pleasure for you if we did things that way? Believe me, you'll be glad we took time to go through all the preliminaries."

"Preliminaries? Such as what?"

"This for starters." He cupped her neck and lowered his lips to hers. Starting soft and sweet, he slowly increased pressure against her mouth.

She sighed into his kiss and he inserted his tongue against hers. Surprised, she would have pulled away, but he held her in place. Caught up in the mysterious sensations showering through her, she soon returned his probing.

He eased her gown down over her hips and legs then tossed it aside. "Now I can see all of you. What a gorgeous woman you are."

Sliding his hand to her breast, he held one orb while he lowered his mouth to the other. When he suckled her peaked nipple, she thought she would come apart. Nothing in her life had ever created such overwhelming desire.

She wanted him to continue forever and pressed his head to her. "That's wonderful."

"Easy, there's more." He slid his hand to her private place and inserted a finger into her. His thumb rubbed a nub.

She thought she might fly off the bed and around the room. Her breathing changed to pants and her head swiveled from side to side. Of its own volition, her body bucked to meet his hand.

He raised over her and she felt that part of him she'd only glimpsed. Surely he was too large. Her breath caught as he slid inside her. He captured her mouth in a kiss. When her barrier broke, sharp pain lasted only a few moments. Then, she met his thrusts with her own.

Faster and faster he drove into her. Higher and higher she climbed until she must be soaring over the tiny cottage. Stars exploded overhead and he cried out his release.

Warmth flowed from him into her that must be his seed. Would she become pregnant this night? With a groan, he sagged against her briefly before he rolled off her. He sighed heavily and threw an arm over her.

She'd hoped for sweet words, but her husband immediately fell asleep. Reasoning he'd worked hard today, somehow she still believed herself cheated. Where were the snuggling, the pillow talk, the shared revelations Stella had mentioned?

While she'd been making love, her husband had been slaking his lust. Anger and humiliation warred within her. What had she expected?

He hadn't asked her to marry him, never professed love. Surely he could have shown more tenderness. Turning away from him, she cried hot tears onto her pillow.

The next morning, she slipped from bed and cleaned herself. When she used the chamber pot, her woman's place between her thighs burned slightly. No wonder, after Josh's fencepost had been inside her.

Drawing on her tan dress and petticoat, she left her feet bare and hurried to start breakfast. Josh had to work today. If he didn't wake soon, she'd have to rouse him. With coffee ready and bacon sizzling, she heard him stirring.

When he came in, his smile beamed at her. "Well, wife, best night's sleep I've had in a while. I hope you slept well."

"Yes, thank you," she lied.

"I hope you're not too sore today. Being as last night was your first time, reckon you might be." He kissed her cheek. "By tonight, you'll be fine."

"Will I?" Her temper flared. All he considered was whether he'd be able to repeat his lust slaking tonight.

He sobered and scratched his jaw. "Leastwise, I reckon so. I've never been with a virgin before, but I tried to make things so you received pleasure too and wouldn't be hurt."

She regretted her anger. "Thank you. I appreciate your gentleness."

After he'd gone, she changed the sheets and had them laundered and hanging on the line when her sister arrived.

Stella came in carrying another package. "I brought you a loaf of bread and some butter." Her sister laid the package on the sideboard. "Well, did the plan work?"

"Yes. He was very happy."

"Why don't you look pleased?"

"I am. I don't know what I expected, but last night fell short."

"Tell me how?"

"He rolled over and went to sleep. No talking, no sweet words, nothing."

"Nettie, he's been sleeping on the sofa, which is at least a foot too short. And that's except the time he slept on the porch. And he'd still worked hard all day. Josh was probably exhausted."

She shrugged, still not placated. "I thought of that."

"Give the relationship time, sister. For heaven's sake, you can't become discouraged after one night. Marriage takes work even when two people love one another the way Finn and I do."

She wrung her hands. "I know you're right. I just…I don't know. I guess I expected more. Josh can be so charming when he wants to. I'd hoped he would want to charm me."

"He will if you give him time to realize how lucky he is."

"But he doesn't think he's lucky, which is one of the problems. Don't you see? He resents me even though his actions caused this marriage."

Stella hugged her. "I repeat, give him time."

Chapter Seven

Josh rode fence with his brother. "No telling what that Tyson will try." He'd kept his handgun with him but his rifle was in the saddle scabbard.

Daniel's eyes scanned the surrounding landscape. "Doesn't make sense he'd target us. He's the one who lost his place. Bank foreclosed. Sheriff held the sale. Why pick on Dad?"

Last night one of the hands, Shorty Dixon, had heard the dogs growl and then spotted Tyson snooping around the barn. The man had escaped into the dark, but everyone was on alert. Shorty and Red Nunn stayed at the house to guard his mother and sister and the buildings. The dogs were with them to sound an alert if strangers were around.

Josh stared at a bunch of cattle near some trees. "You can't reason with a man who's crazy from drink and regret. I reckon he's lost his mind."

"What are you staring at?"

"Look at the edge of those cows. You see anything odd?"

Daniel adjusted the brim of his hat. "Appears one's down."

Josh urged Spartan into a gallop. Daniel on his horse, Sport, raced beside him. As they drew close, Josh realized the shape wasn't right for a cow at the same time he caught the glint of metal.

"Duck, it's a trap!"

A rifle shot cut the spring air. A horse screamed and fell, taking Daniel with him. Josh seized his own rifle and leapt from the saddle. Firing at the mysterious shape as he ran, he raced toward his younger brother.

Daniel lay with his left leg trapped beneath Sport. "Leg's penned but I'm okay. Go get the bastard."

Josh mounted Spartan and kneed him into a gallop

toward the source of the shot. As he rode, he fired repeatedly at the shape. When he reached what had resembled a downed cow, he discovered a barrel on its side. From the depression in the grass, someone had lain in wait for some time.

He wanted to take off tracking the sidewinder, but his brother was trapped under a dead horse. Was Daniel really all right or did he have a broken leg? Reluctant to let a bushwhacker escape, Josh turned his horse to check on Daniel.

"He got away." Josh dismounted and was at Daniel's side with a canteen.

His brother didn't respond.

Josh dribbled water on his brother's face in an attempt to revive him. "Talk to me."

He shook Daniel's shoulder. "You said you were all right." He heard the panicked sob in his voice.

First thing, Josh needed to get the dead horse off his brother's leg. He fired three quick shots into the air, careful to direct them where the shots wouldn't fall to earth on anything living. With luck, some of the hands would hear the sound and came to investigate.

Spartan shied from the dead animal. Josh looped his lasso around Spartan's pommel and then tied the other end to that of Sport. "Go on, boy, pull him up. More, a little more. That's a good boy, Spartan."

Carefully, Josh slid his brother's leg from beneath the carcass. From the awkward angles, Josh figured the leg was broken in a couple of places. Daniel moaned but didn't regain consciousness.

When his injured sibling was free, Josh left his brother long enough to remove the rope that held Sport and the body fell back to the ground. After removing the rope from his horse's pommel, he coiled it and returned it to its place on the saddle.

He patted his own horse on the neck. "Good boy, Spartan. I know that was hard for you."

Lord, help us. Help me get Daniel to safety.

No one was in sight to help but he had to get Daniel home. Josh stripped the saddle and gear from Sport. Using the bedroll as a travois might work. With the freed end of his rope, he tied one end of the bedroll tightly. Using the saddle blanket for extra cushion, he placed his own bedroll on top of Daniel's

After gently lifting Daniel atop the bed, he set Spartan toward home trailing the hastily-fashioned travois carrying his unconscious brother. Josh had to walk beside the makeshift bed to prevent the contraption from flipping or Daniel from rolling off.

He looked back to find buzzards already circling poor Sport's body. Damn, his brother loved that horse. If he did nothing else this month, he would repay Bob Tyson for this cowardly outrage.

After at least six hours, buildings signaling home came into view. Josh could tell the second Shorty spotted him because the man shouted and Red hopped on a horse and came running.

When he drew near, Red sized up the situation. "Wait right here 'fore you keel over. I'll get the wagon."

Josh dropped to the ground. He pushed back his brother's hair. "Sorry this was so hard on you, little brother. Won't be long now before you're safe in your room with Mama tending your leg."

Daniel's skin was hot to the touch. No telling how many miles away they'd been when they'd been bushwhacked, but getting here had taken most of the day. The rumble of a wagon captured Josh's attention. He wasn't surprised to see his mother on the seat with Red or to see Shorty and Rebecca riding in back.

The second the wagon stopped, Mama was out and hurrying toward them. "What happened?"

Josh related the events. "Didn't see who shot at us, but I can guess."

Mama's eyes blazed with anger. "I hope the coward rots in hell. No call to shoot from hiding. No call to shoot at all."

She looked up to meet his gaze. "You look fit to drop. Get in the wagon."

"Thanks, Mama, but I'll ride Spartan and brush him down. He sure didn't like pulling a travois, but he did to please me. Sensed this was an emergency."

"Of course he did, he's a smart horse. Shorty, Red, help me get Daniel onto the wagon. Becky, when the men lift your brother, you and I will get those bedrolls laid out so Daniel can lay on them."

Pa and Chuck Jones rode up as the wagon pulled near the back door. Pa was off his horse and running toward them. Shorty and Red carried Daniel into the house and upstairs to his room.

"What's happened to Daniel?" Pa clutched at his shoulder. "Son, are you all right? You look about ready to drop."

Exactly how he felt. Plus, he wanted to sit and bawl but McClintock men were tougher than that. He pulled himself up straight. "Bushwhacker caught us in the back corner. Sport's dead, crushed Daniel's leg falling." Once again he explained what had happened, but in more detail.

Chuck took Spartan's reins from his hand and gathered the reins from the two he and Pa had ridden. "I'll see to all the horses."

"Thanks. Mine deserves extra oats tonight." Josh let his father guide him into the house.

Face streaked with tears, Rebecca ran down the steps and into the kitchen. "Josh, Mama said for you to stay until she can check you. I have to go tell Nettie 'cause if she sees one of the hands come it'll scare her half to death."

"Pa, whoever shot Daniel is still out there. You think Becky oughta be riding alone?"

Rebecca wiped at her cheeks and sent him a glare. "I can take care of myself. I know how to ride fast and shoot."

"I know you do, sweetheart." Pa met his gaze and hugged Rebecca to him. "Josh wasn't alone and that still didn't help. Just the same, I reckon someone ought to go with you."

Shorty and Red entered the kitchen in time to overhear.

Shorty said, "I told Miss Kathryn I'd ride with Miss Rebecca, boss. I'm not as young as I used to be, but I'm still a good shot."

Pa clapped the man on the shoulder. "Thanks, Shorty. I'd go but I'd like to check on my boy." He pointed at his daughter. "Becky, you be careful and heed what Shorty says."

She headed for the door. "I will, Pa."

"Good." He turned and slung an arm across Josh's shoulders. "Let's go check on your brother."

When they were in the room, Josh was shocked to see Daniel still unconscious. Mama looked up. "Red's going for the doctor. I could set his leg, but I think Doctor Sullivan can do a better job. He's awfully bruised from the fall and getting here."

Josh dropped into a chair. "This is my fault. I should have known there wasn't a cow down. There wasn't a buzzard in sight."

Pa stood by him. "No, this isn't your fault. You figured out how to get your brother home with him unconscious. That back corner is four miles from the house over rough ground. Surprised the bedrolls didn't shred before you got here."

"We left a trail of cloth and padding, Pa. Daniel's is ruined. I think mine survived."

Mama looked at him. "Son, I suggested Nettie come here. You and she can sleep in your old room. I'd feel a lot better with all my kids here and safe."

He reared back and stared at his mother. "We can't live here."

She stretched out her hand and touched his knee. "Just for tonight. A few days at most."

Pa pulled her into his arms. "Everything will be all right, Kathryn my love."

"I hope you're right. Whoever did this has to be clever and crazy. You can't reason with someone like that. There's no telling what he might do next. I-I'd like my family where we can watch over and help one another."

She held Pa's hand as she sat back beside Daniel. "Red's going to alert Dallas after he starts Doctor Sullivan on his way here."

Pa went to the window and peered outside. "Buster and Marty ought to have been back by now. If they're not in by the time Nettie gets here, we'll have to go looking for them."

Josh sat with his elbows on his knees and cradled his head with his hands. "I wish you hadn't bought that land, Pa."

He looked up. "Sorry, Pa. I'm just upset about Daniel

getting hurt. I know you bought Tyson's place so Daniel and I would both have enough to support us when you and Mama retire. That's a long time from now."

"Not often a place joining ours comes up for sale, son. I didn't think I could pass up the opportunity. Now I wish I had."

Mama looked from him to Pa. "Both of you stop talking like that. Tyson will be caught and Daniel will heal. Then you'll both feel differently."

Josh wasn't so sure. Looking at his brother lying so still and lifeless sent chills down his spine. If only he'd realized they headed for a trap sooner. If only he'd hit the sorry sonofabitch who shot Sport. If only Sport hadn't fallen on Daniel.

If only, if only, if only…

His mind replayed every second of the disaster.

Mama bathed Daniel's face and neck with one of her soothing remedies. She glanced at Pa who still looked out the window. "Do you see any sign of Becky and Nettie?"

Josh stood. "Hasn't been long enough, Mama. Takes me fifteen minutes to ride here each morning. Plus, Nettie will have to pack some of our things."

Emma, their plump housekeeper and cook, came in carrying a teapot and cups on a tray. "I made you a nice pot of tea." She looked at Pa. "I've got fresh coffee in the kitchen and supper will be served soon as the others get here."

Chapter Eight

Nettie had supper ready when she heard hoof beats. She listened. Sounded like several horses, so she rushed to the window.

When Rebecca and one of the hands climbed off their horses with a riderless horse along, she had to grab the sill to keep from falling. What had happened to Josh? The hand, whose name she thought was Shorty, stayed with the horses.

Tears streaming down her face, Rebecca rushed onto the porch. "Don't be upset, Josh is all right. Daniel's been hurt."

Relief washed over her that Josh was okay along with guilt that she would experience that sensation with poor Daniel injured.

Hand at her throat, she asked, "That Tyson person?"

"We think so." Her sister-in-law wiped at her tears.

"Is Daniel all right?"

Rebecca gulped, as if stifling a sob. "We don't know. His leg's broken in a couple of places and he's unconscious."

Nettie hugged the girl's shoulders. "I know Kathryn is skilled at helping the sick. Does she set bones too?"

"Not usually. Red's gone for the doctor and to warn Dallas and Cenora."

"So you think everyone named McClintock is in danger."

"Mama and Pa do, and so does Josh. Mama wants you to pack some things for you and Josh and come to our house for a few days. She's afraid you're a target here, especially during the day."

Target? She hadn't considered that she might be in danger due to being married to a McClintock. "I'll hurry. Could you pack up the meat and our supper to take with us? Otherwise, the food will spoil."

Nettie hurried to the bedroom and pulled the valise

from under the bed. She didn't own many clothes to toss into the bag. Sad when the husband had more clothes than the wife. Of course, him working with cattle and brush, she imagined he ruined clothes a lot faster than she did. She included Josh's things and shoved the case closed.

By the time she returned to the small kitchen area, Rebecca had a basket of food packed and ready to travel.

The girl smiled tremulously and gestured to the sink of soapy water. "I didn't get the pans washed for you. If you want to take time to wash, I'll dry."

Nettie plunged her hands into the water and scrubbed a skillet. "Since they belong to Mr. Tall Trees, I'd better see they're clean and put away before I leave. I hope he doesn't mind us living here."

Becky dried a pan. "He's a real nice man. You'll like him. Everyone but Gran does. No matter what we say to her, Gran still thinks all Indians are heathens."

"If you ask me, that man Tyson is the real heathen."

As the two of them worked quickly, Nettie had dozens of questions. For most, Rebecca had no answer.

Nettie located a sheet of paper and pencil. "I'd better leave a note in case some of my family come by and wonder they I'm not here."

She tacked the paper to the front door. Within minutes she and her young sister-in-law were on the horses and riding astride in spite of their skirts.

Shorty instructed them, "You stay behind me but close-like. Whoever shot Daniel's horse is crazy, so we have to go easy."

Nettie thought she might jump out of her skin. They had to ride through brush, trees, and up and down areas where an ambusher might lie in wait. She knew Shorty was wary, but she felt exposed. Were they targets?

Only married a week and she'd already had a month of trouble. Immediately, she was sorry for her selfish thoughts. Her home hadn't been vandalized and her brother Lance wasn't lying unconscious and injured.

Josh and his parents must be weighed down with worry. All from a man who held the McClintocks responsible for his bad judgment. Surely Sheriff Yates could do something.

Dusk had fallen when they rode into the large homestead's grounds and pulled up at the kitchen door. Josh and another man came to help them. Her husband helped her dismount.

He held her against him and nestled his cheek against her hair. "Glad you hurried. I was afraid that maniac would shoot you."

"How's Daniel?" She clung to him and he cradled her near. Was he really worried about her? A spark of hope seeped into her soul.

He broke the embrace to unfasten the valise and carry the case for her. "Doc only got here a couple of minutes before you did."

She fell into stride with him.

"I haven't been this worried since Dallas went silent at the Lost Maples pass. No, this is worse because Daniel is my baby brother."

With her arm around his waist, they walked up the steps. "I know how worried I'd be if Lance were injured. But Dallas is fine now. Between your mother and the doctor, I'll bet Daniel will soon be all right."

His voice shuddered, "Dear Lord in Heaven, I pray you're right."

Rebecca carried the basket and set it on the kitchen table. "Y'all go on and I'll put the food away. We'll have something to eat soon."

Emma brushed a stray lock of brown hair into her bun then lifted the cloth covering the contents. "That's right, Becky. No matter what happens to folks, they have to eat."

Rebecca said, "I need to see about Daniel."

The housekeeper shook her head. "You stay here, Becky, and help me so you're not underfoot upstairs. I know you're worried, but there's no change since you saw him. We'll have a lot of folks to feed. You can see your brother later."

He and Nettie climbed the stairs together.

Nettie said, "Your sister said you had to walk a long ways after Daniel was hurt. Are you all right?"

He gave her a weak grin. "Tired and already getting

sore. Cowboys don't walk much unless they're stringing fence. Even branding, we stay mainly in one place. Mostly, I'm worried out of my mind."

He guided her down a hall and opened a door. "This was my room and where we'll sleep while we're here. I hope this is all right."

She gazed around the spacious room. At least there was a very large bed. She tried not to think about tonight when she'd share that bed with this man.

"What a nice place. And nice large windows."

"I'll raise them so the room can air out. Don't think it's been used this week."

She sat on a straight-back chair. "Hard to believe all that's happened since we wed, isn't it? Only one week, but it seems months have passed."

"Well, if you'd like to settle in, I'll check on Daniel."

"Do you mind if I leave unpacking for later and go with you? I mean, I'm not really a family member, but I like Daniel very much."

He gave her a perplexed stare. "Of course you're a part of this clan. You're my wife. This will be our home someday, unless you want a newer one."

"I love this house. I only meant that we're barely married and you weren't that happy about having to wed me. For that reason, I don't feel…well, like a *real* wife."

He grasped her shoulders and met her gaze. "Nettie, I may be an ass sometimes, but I take marriage seriously. I…I've had a hard time dealing with all that happened last weekend, but I'll find my way if you give me time."

She offered a genuine smile. "I have a lot of time. Will fifty or sixty years be enough?"

He returned her grin. "Reckon it might. Let's see if the doctor's finished examining Daniel."

***

Josh stood just inside his brother's room while Mama and Pa helped the doctor set Daniel's leg.

Doctor Sullivan glanced up. "Broken in three places. Sorry, but I fear he'll have a limp."

Mama's face was taut and he didn't know how she held

up so well in times of trouble. "I'll make sure he has the herbs to help his bones knit."

"I know you will, Kathryn. If anyone alive can speed his recovery, you're that person. Now, let's turn him over real easy-like and see about his back and head."

Josh strode to the bed. "I'll help."

When they rolled his brother to his side, they exposed a nasty gouge and bruises.

Doc cleaned and treated the gash before applying a bandage. Afterward, he probed carefully along Daniel's spine and up to the back of his head. Finally, he nodded and gestured for them to let his brother roll onto his back again.

"Kathryn, you know how to care for that cut as well as I do. Probably a rock he fell onto knifed into him." The kindly doctor slowly returned his supplies to his satchel.

When he'd closed the bag, he faced them. "I'm not sure how damaged Daniel is. I can't tell you how I hate to give you my diagnosis. Looks to me like his spine's broken and he may be paralyzed from the waist down."

"No," Mama cried. "He's only twenty." She choked on her sobs.

Pa pulled her into his arms, but he looked ready to break into tears as well.

The verdict hit Josh like a blow to his gut and his legs wanted to give up on him. Nettie appeared at his side and slid her arm around his waist. Right now, having her support was good.

Pa's voice broke as he asked, "You're sure?"

Doc shook his head. "Can't be until he wakes up. Human spirit has a lot to do with recovery. Daniel's a strong young man, both mentally and physically."

The physician picked up his bag. "Even if he is paralyzed, may only be temporary. Just wanted to prepare you. Your reaction can affect his recovery. He needs positive words and no mollycoddling or pity. You can't let on you think he's doomed to a useless life. "

Doc gave a dismissive wave. "You're smart folks and I reckon you know all that. Doesn't hurt to have someone remind you is all."

Pa extended his hand. "Thank you, Doc. Appreciate your honesty."

"I can see myself out. You folks get some food in you and have someone sit with Daniel. May wake soon and need some nourishment, especially water. Dribble some into his mouth if he isn't awake in an hour."

Josh shook the doc's hand. "We will."

"Man who came for me told me what you did to get your brother home. Mighty good thinking. If his back's broken like I think, loading him on a horse would have paralyzed him for sure—maybe killed him." He clapped Josh on the shoulder and left the room.

Josh sat on the floor and rested his head on his knees. He'd almost tied Daniel to the saddle and tried to hold him upright while he mounted behind him.

Thank you, God, for giving me the idea of a travois.

Mama said, "You heard Doctor Sullivan. Go down and eat."

Nettie walked over and hugged Mama. "No, Kathryn. You're half sick from worry. I'll sit with Daniel and bathe his face occasionally. You go down and sit at the table with your husband and son."

His mother shook her head. "I couldn't eat a bite."

Gently, Nettie turned Mama and guided her toward the door. "You have to for the sake of Daniel and others. You're the healer. We can't afford for you to get sick."

Mama hugged Nettie. "I knew you'd be a wonderful daughter-in-law. You'll let us know if there's the slightest change?"

Nettie gave his mother a smile. "Of course. I'll yell my head off."

Pa put his arm around Mama and they left the room.

He met Nettie's gaze. "Thanks." What else could he say?

She motioned him to stand. "You, too, Josh. You had a horrible day. Eat and then turn in. I'll sit with Daniel for a while."

He knew she was right. Even rising from the floor was almost more than he could manage. "I'll bring you a plate of dinner."

She smiled and made a shooing motion. "Go on, husband."

He managed to stand. "Hard to remember I'm the head of the household."

"I'll keep reminding you," she said as he left the room.

Chapter Nine

Nettie returned to sit beside her brother-in-law. How young he appeared lying there still and limp as a rag doll. She wrung excess water from the cloth and bathed his face and neck, then his hands.

Emma appeared with a plate of food and mug of coffee. "Nice of you to sit with him, Miss Nettie. I can watch while you eat."

"No, thank you, Emma. And I'm just plain Nettie. I can manage nicely. You have a lot to do downstairs. Has Kathryn calmed any?"

Emma set the tray beside Nettie and then walked around to the other side of the bed. "A bit. They're making plans and that's redirected her mind."

The housekeeper brushed Daniel's hair gently from his forehead. "I came here when he was just a toddler. Into everything he was, but such a good boy. All you had to do was tell him 'no' and he moved on to something else. Like as not, he got another 'no' there too."

"Sounds like you have a special tenderness for him."

Emma's brown eyes misted over but she smiled. "I try not to be partial, but this boy just captured my heart. Don't get the wrong idea. Josh and Dallas were good boys and I think the world of both of them. Becky is sweet and kind enough no one could find fault with her."

"I understand. My younger brother Lance is only slightly older than Rebecca. I can't help feeling a special…I guess you'd call it protectiveness for him even though my older sister Stella and I are very close. In fact, Stella has always been my best friend. Still, you can't control your heart, can you?"

"No, and that's the truth. Well, if you're sure I'm not needed here, I'd better get back to my kitchen."

Nettie ate a few bites between bathing Daniel's face. When he moved his right arm, she almost ran to the door to call

Josh. No, better to wait and see if Daniel would open his eyes.

After setting her plate aside, she massaged his hands and temples. Why she did so, she couldn't explain. Perhaps she worked from instinct—or desperation.

Alternating bathing his face with massage of his temple and head and hands, she continued working. Her brief conversation with Emma had set her thinking. What would she do if this had happened to Lance? She could imagine the terror clutching the hearts of Daniel's family.

While she was massaging his hand, Daniel's fingers wrapped around hers.

She touched his cheek. "Daniel? Daniel, can you hear me?"

His eyelids fluttered but didn't open completely.

Quickly, she bathed his face. "Daniel, wake up. You need to open your eyes and look at me. Come on, show me your kind blue eyes."

He whispered, "Can't."

"Yes, you can, Daniel. Open your eyes and look at me."

This time his eyelids opened and fright radiated from his gaze. "Nettie? Can't move my legs."

What could she tell him? She wasn't the one to give him the bad news. Brushing her hand across his forehead, she chose her words carefully. "Of course you can't. You had an accident but Josh got you home. Doctor Sullivan has been here and will return tomorrow. Your left leg is broken and splinted and there's a bad gash on your back."

She rose. "Excuse me, I promised to tell everyone when you regained consciousness."

In the hall outside his room she hurried to the head of the stairs and called, "Daniel's awake."

At once, she heard the sound of running footsteps. Kathryn led the group of people up the stairs. Austin, Josh, and Becky were right behind her. Nettie chewed her lip and waited in the hallway.

Josh stopped beside her. "He say anything?"

She kept her voice low. "Said he couldn't move his legs. I-I didn't think I should tell him why. That needs to come from your parents and the doctor."

Josh stuffed his hands in his pockets. "Yeah, poor guy. He'll be devastated."

"There are enough people in that room already. Please tell them I can stay up and sit with Daniel tonight."

"I'll let them know when I check on him."

She touched hand. "Josh, remember to be cheerful. And then I hope you'll go to bed."

He offered a sad grin. "There you go, wife, forgetting who's head of the household."

"Oh, I haven't forgotten, husband. In this case it's your father." She punctuated her statement with a light punch to his arm.

Josh composed his face and strode to Daniel's side. "About time you woke up."

Daniel's face showed he'd been crying but he smiled. "Thanks for dragging me home. I hear that's literally what you did."

"Couldn't leave you for the buzzards and coyotes. Would have been a terrible thing to do to the wildlife. Imagine their indigestion would have killed 'em."

His brother sobered. "Looks like you'll have my share of the work to do from now on."

Josh shook his head. "Nonsense. You think I'll let you lay around here for long, you're mistaken. You'll get your lazy rear out of bed soon and be back helping me or I'll drag you out of here for sure."

He turned to his mother. "My wife has ordered me to go to bed, but let me take a turn sitting up with this lay-about tonight. Just rap on the door. Nettie sleeps like a stone, so don't worry about bothering her, although she said she'd be happy to stay up all night with Daniel."

"That's all right, son. Pa and I will probably take turns until Doctor Sullivan comes tomorrow."

Pa walked him to the door and into the hall then touched his shoulder. "You'll understand when you have your own children. Your mother and I couldn't sleep a wink right now."

Josh wondered if he and Nettie would have kids. They hadn't started off well and he knew she still hadn't forgiven him for being forced to marry him. She let him take her virginity last night, but she hadn't been happy with him this morning when they awoke. He didn't understand why. He'd never had complaints about pleasing a woman before.

He closed his old bedroom's door behind him.

His wife sat with her hands folded in her lap, still wearing her clothes. "I stayed dressed in case I need to sit with Daniel."

He shook his head. "Mama and Pa said they want to. I feel awful about Daniel's diagnosis. Guess if he were my son, I'd be inconsolable."

"At least he's home and safe, thanks to you."

He sat on the edge of the bed and took off his boots. "If I weren't so ragged, I'd insist on staying up. Don't think I could stay awake all night."

"Better to sleep now and then help out tomorrow. I imagine your father won't want to leave the house."

Exhaling a whoosh of breath, he stood and shucked out of his clothes. "Guess you're right. Buster and Marty didn't get in until we were eating supper. Buster said there were more fences cut and he ran late repairing them."

She rose from the chair. "Don't think about it now, Josh. Go to bed and sleep. You've had a terrible day and need the rest."

Feeling several times his age, he crawled into bed. "Yeah, one thing Daniel said is right. I'll be working harder to fill in for him and I reckon Pa will be missing work for a while."

"Before I turn in, I'm going to speak to your mother and try to convince her to let me sit with Daniel while she rests."

"That mean you don't want me touching you again?"

She turned to face him. "It means I think your mother needs a break. If she says no, then I'll be right back."

"Guess you can try, but Mama is the hovering type. Don't think she'll leave Daniel. I already tried."

He crossed his arms beneath his head and looked at her with half-closed eyes. She had taken the pins from her hair and must have brushed those golden locks. She sure had pretty hair.

In fact, she truly was a beautiful woman in looks and by nature.

"I'll probably be back in a few minutes. I have to try or I couldn't sleep."

"Okay, I'll be here waiting for you."

She slipped out the door and closed it softly behind her. Nothing about her was like other women he'd known. He couldn't figure her out at all.

***

Quietly, Nettie entered Daniel's room. Kathryn was alone with her sleeping youngest son.

In a whisper, Nettie said, "I hoped you'd let me sit with him while you get some rest."

Her mother-in-law smiled at her. "I don't think I could sleep, but you're kind to offer. Austin will take over for me about two, but I still won't be able to leave Daniel."

"I know his injury is a shock. He's young and healthy and I believe he'll walk again. You have to have faith in Daniel's determination."

"I'm trying. What you say is the same as I'd tell someone in this case. Since this happened to my son, though, I'm so worried I'm having trouble being positive.

Nettie decided to give one last try. "You know, you should get some sleep in case someone needs your medical help."

Kathryn stared sadly at Daniel before meeting Nettie's gaze. "They'll have to depend on Doctor Sullivan. Family comes first."

Nettie peered around the spacious room. "Kathryn, you should have a cot or bed moved in here. Then you could stretch out and rest even if you couldn't sleep.

"That's a good suggestion. I'll have Austin arrange for one. Now, you go on and get some sleep, Nettie. No doubt I'll need your help in the coming days. Bless you for being such a kind woman."

Nettie hugged her mother-in-law. "Thank you. Hearing you saying that means a lot to me."

"I mean what I said, dear. Now, shoo." Kathryn gestured towards the door.

Nettie smiled at the generous and gracious woman she

so admired. "If you're certain, then I'll go to bed."

When she got back into the bedroom she and Josh would share—his former room—he was asleep. She had to admit relief. Quietly, she changed into her gown and crawled between the covers, careful not to awaken her husband.

How odd that sounded. Her husband. He mumbled in his sleep and rolled toward her. His arm lay across her waist and he leaned into her hair. His deep breathing in her ear assured her he remained asleep.

In spite of knowing his true feelings, lying cuddled in his arms created a sense of well-being, as if she were treasured and protected. If only he actually felt that way about her. Would he ever change his opinion?

Sleep beckoned and she drifted toward slumber, only to be startled by her husband.

He pulled her close. "Glad you're finally here."

"I was only in your brother's room a few minutes. Guess you were too worn out from your day to stay awake."

After planting a kiss to her shoulder, he said, "I'm not asleep now."

His manhood pressed into her hip and his hands were everywhere, leaving burning trails that ignited her.

She grabbed his hands and hissed, "Your mother is right across the hall. Your sister is next door. Surely you don't intend us to…you know, while we're here in your parents' home."

He leaned in to nuzzle her neck. "Of course I do. Not that anyone will know or care what we do because we're married."

She couldn't help squirming as his kisses heated her skin. "But they'll hear us and know what we're doing. How could I face them tomorrow?"

His hands cupped her breasts that suddenly seemed to have grown heavier and ached for his touch. "Naw, they won't hear. We can be quiet. I'll show you."

Curiosity and desire filled her. She visualized his mother across the hall, his sister next door and cringed. By now, his father was probably with his mother and brother, too. She pushed away Josh's hands.

"Your brother is lying paralyzed in pain and all you can think about is us coming together? What is wrong with you?"

"You know what? Aw, hell, never mind." He rolled over with his back to her.

Torn by her decision, she raised her hand to touch his bare shoulder. No, she couldn't go through with pulling him back to her. Somehow, she didn't think doing so would be respectful of his family's situation. Yet, not doing so widened the breech between her and Josh.

She wanted to curl into a knot and bawl, but she couldn't give in. Drawing fortitude from her resolve to be a stronger woman, she plumped her pillow and turned her back on her husband. Respectful of her in-laws she might be, but she sure didn't feel satisfied.

Chapter Ten

When Josh peeked in on Daniel the next morning, his sister sat beside the bed reading. She looked up and smiled and put a finger to her lips. Daniel was asleep.

Josh went down to breakfast and found Sheriff Yates seated at the kitchen table sipping coffee. He sat across from the sheriff.

Josh picked up the steaming mug Emma set in front of him and took a sip before he said, "Glad to see you, Sheriff. Did I miss news about Tyson?"

The sheriff leaned forward. "I was just telling your folks here that I'm going to arrest that man today. Have word where he's holed up not far from here."

"You care if I tag along?" Josh filled his plate and dug into scrambled eggs, biscuits, and bacon.

His father sent him a steely glare. "Now, son, don't go riding off to get revenge. I've one son in trouble and don't need to double that."

Josh was determined to go and met his father's gaze. "You going?" He forked another bite.

His pa nodded. "We're waiting for the rest of the posse to join us here."

"Pa, I know you're worried about Daniel but that doesn't mean you can wrap me in cotton wool. I'd sure like to see Tyson arrested and taken to jail for what he's done." He figured he'd better eat fast if a posse was on the way.

Mama touched Pa's sleeve. "Austin, I worry as much as you do, maybe more because I'm a mother, but think how you'd feel if you were Josh."

His father raked his fingers through his dark hair just touched by gray at the sides. "Reckon you're right, Kathryn. I sure want to see that sorry sonofab..gun pay for what he's done."

They ate in silence. Soon, the pound of horses' hooves

outside sent the men to their feet. Josh swallowed a last gulp of coffee, snatched a couple more biscuits, and followed his father and the sheriff.

His mother called after them, "Be careful."

They stopped so Pa could talk with his foreman, Buster.

"Leave Shorty and Chuck in or near the house in case Tyson gets away. I want Red and Marty near the barn. Each of you keep your guns handy."

Buster stood with hands at his side. "Don't worry, boss. This place will be all right. Just like you asked, I sent word to town last night that Miss Kathryn can't make calls on anyone until this is over." He gestured to Josh's cousin. "Dallas sent three of his men to help us and they're keeping watch on the ridge above the house."

"Let's hope today sees the end of this trouble." Pa climbed on his horse. He yelled, "Stay, boys," at the two jumping and barking dogs.

Both dogs obeyed but their grumbling left no doubt they wanted to accompany the horses.

Filled with rage and anguish, Josh mounted Spartan. He couldn't rid his mind of the image of Daniel after his brother had learned about the paralysis. Capturing Tyson wouldn't help Daniel—he wasn't sure anything would, but having the man in jail sure as hell would make Josh feel better.

He rode beside his cousin. "You leave Cenora and the baby on their own?"

Dallas leaned back in the saddle. "You crazy? I left Xavier and two others at the house guarding them plus both dogs are there."

He held up a hand in protest. "I meant was Cenora at home or her parents' place."

"Sorry to snap at you. Guess we're all on edge. Figured she'd be safer at home with several of the hands and both dogs keeping watch. Guess I should have had her parents come to the house, too."

Sheriff Yates led them across the range. When they reached the gate leading to the land previously owned by Tyson, the sheriff halted them.

"From here on, we have to ride quiet." He looked at

Deputy William Bishop, who'd dismounted to open the gate. Bishop was locally teased about his custom of wearing fancy spurs. "Thanks for not wearing your spurs."

Yates raised his hand. "No talking and walk the horses. We're headed for that line of trees. There's a cabin back in the woods and I want to surround the place before those inside know we're there."

When they'd traveled into the trees for about ten minutes, they spotted a small shack. Smoke drifted from the chimney flue. Three saddled horses stood in a nearby lean-to. Yates dismounted and wrapped his reins around a branch. The other men followed suit.

The sheriff signaled for them to split and circle the cabin. Josh went with his father, Dallas, and Deputy Lester Higgins. They circled to the north until they had a view that would expose anyone leaving the front or back of the cabin. Deputy Bishop and three men from town circled south. Each appeared to have chosen protective cover.

When they were in place, Sheriff Yates called, "You're surrounded, Tyson. Come out with your hands up."

Glass shattered and a shotgun blast answered.

Yates shouted, "Don't be a fool, Tyson. You're surrounded and can't escape. No point committing suicide."

Another discharge sent splinters from a tree showering the sheriff.

He raised a hand. "All right, men, close in."

Cautiously, Josh edged forward.

When he would have run toward the cabin, Dallas grabbed his arm. "Don't make yourself a target. Let's capture the scalawag without any of us getting killed."

Josh grinned at his cousin. "That'd be my first choice. Need to close in, though, and drive him into the open."

Lester called, "Cover me. I'm moving in closer."

Josh, his father, and Dallas fired while Lester darted from tree to tree. The deputy reached the side of the shack. Josh saw the walls spattered with holes from their bullets. The thin clapboard offered little protection.

Dallas was the best shot in the family. He took careful aim and shot the man at the window. The criminal's gun flew from his hand and he screamed in pain.

Josh's father said, "Good shot. You hit his hand. That one will live to go to trial if he's smart enough to give up now."

A hail of bullets from the other side ended.

Sheriff Yates called, "This is your last chance. Come out with your hands up or you'll come out dead."

The door slowly opened and a dirty, once-white handkerchief waved before three men came out. One limped and had a bandana tied around his leg. The one Dallas hit had wrapped a handkerchief around his hand, but blood ran down his up-stretched arm. Tyson appeared to be unharmed.

Quickly, the men were handcuffed and loaded onto their horses. Tyson cursed and ranted the entire time. He blamed the McClintocks for his wife leaving, his financial woes, and for him losing his ranch. Obviously the man had slipped past sanity and into a world only he knew.

Relief lightened the burden Josh had carried since Daniel was injured. Anger still burned in him that Tyson acted so reprehensibly, but at least the man would do no more damage. Now Tyson would pay for his crimes. And a side benefit that occurred to Josh was that now he and Nettie could return to the Tall Trees cabin and she would once again share her body.

Josh congratulated himself on today's outcome but then he noticed his father's arm dripped blood. He grabbed his father. "Pa, why didn't you mention you were hit?"

"Didn't have time." He removed the bandana from his neck and handed it to Josh. "Tie this up for me, will you, son? Your mother will fix me right up soon as we're home."

Josh did his best to staunch the blood. Already Pa had grown pale and the tautness of his face testified to his pain. They retrieved their horses and rode for town. As they passed the ranch house, Dallas accompanied Josh and his pa as they peeled off and went to let his family know what had happened.

Shorty came to take their reins and care for the horses. Dallas walked on one side and Josh on the other and ushered his father into the kitchen. Emma was at the table kneading dough. His mother stood at the range, stirring a pot of what smelled like chili.

She turned when they entered. "Thank Heavens, you're back."

"Mama, Pa needs doctoring." Josh guided his father to the chair Dallas pulled around for him.

His mother rushed toward them. "Austin, what's happened?"

Her eyes like saucers, Rebecca cried, "Pa?"

Recovering her composure, the girl said, "I'll get the doctoring bag." She rushed out of the room.

Pa raised his uninjured hand as if to stay their fears. "Nothing to take on about. Bullet went through my arm. Least I hope it did."

Before he could offer another word, his mother had untied the bandanas and ripped off the sleeve to examine the wound. The fabric was soaked with blood and a wide trail of the sticky life-substance ran onto his denim pants.

"No exit wound. I'll have to get the lead out. You want me to work on you here or with you lying down upstairs?"

Pa gave a slight shake of his head. "Don't think I can make it up the stairs. Starting to feel a little light-headed."

Dallas dipped until his shoulder was under Pa's undamaged arm and then he stood, taking Pa up with him. "Josh and I can get you to your bed, Uncle Austin. You'll be more comfortable there."

Rebecca reappeared with the medical bag Mama used for house calls.

While his mother gathered additional items, he and Dallas helped Pa to his room. Before now, Josh had never seen his father so willing to accept help. Worry gripped Josh's gut in a vise.

He pushed his pa's fingers aside and unbuttoned the blood-stained garment. Dallas turned down the cover and Pa sat on the mattress.

"Kathryn won't want the bedding stained."

She entered the room. "Austin McClintock, you get those clothes off and lie down. You think fabric is more important than you are? Since when have my priorities been so upside down?"

"Never, dear, but I know you set store by things being clean." He peered at his fingers. "Hand's not working right."

Rebecca carried the old sheets used to pad and protect. She laid them out so that they covered the area where their father would rest his injured arm. "All ready, Pa. I'll go tell Nettie and Daniel what's happened while you get into bed."

Dallas said, "Uncle Austin, we'll help. If you can unbutton your pants, we'll shuck you out of them and your boots."

When his father was tucked into bed, Mama started her ministrations with Rebecca assisting. Not for the first time, Josh noted how efficiently his mother worked and how his sister appeared to anticipate her needs. No wonder their services were in great demand by people in the community.

In case he was needed, Josh stood to one side with Dallas. Sweat beaded Pa's face as he bit down on a folded cloth.

Mama worked to dig out the lead. "Sorry, Austin. The bullet's into the bone. Miracle your arm wasn't shattered. I'm sure the bone's fractured."

Sweat beaded on his father's brow. The gash required stitches before bandaging.

When she'd finished, Mama leaned over and kissed Papa on the forehead. "This should be splinted, but I need to be able to dress the wound twice each day."

With his uninjured hand, Pa twined his fingers with Mama's. "Know I'm in good hands, Kathryn. Have to admit I hurt like hell."

She administered laudanum. "You'll sleep now and that will help you heal. Later, I'll bring you something to eat."

Josh laid a hand on his father's good shoulder. "I'll sit here in case you need anything, Pa."

Pa tried to move his injured arm and grimaced. "Thanks, but you go on down to supper. Reckon Kathryn will see I'm all right soon enough."

Seeing his father flat on his back and pale was like a punch on the jaw. He forced what he hoped was a jovial tone. "Got that right. She'll make sure you get well with no complications."

Another grimace let him know Pa was in pain. "Sorry, son. With Daniel laid up and me out of commission for a couple of days, we've heaped work on you."

"Don't think like that. You'll be up and around soon."

"Might need to hire another hand."

"Aw, I figure we can manage now that Tyson's locked up."

"Yeah, we'll see how work goes. You go on now. Your mother gave me something that's made me sleepy. Believe I'll have a nap."

Josh left his father's room and quietly closed the door. At least his father's injury wasn't as debilitating as Daniel's, but seeing his father lying in bed shook Josh to his core. Pa was the family's backbone, the problem solver.

Merciful God in Heaven, protect this family from further harm.

He stood in the hall in a daze. Nettie left his brother's room.

She came up to him and grasped his arm. "Dallas wants to sit with Daniel a while. Come down with me and let's eat together."

"Good of you to stay with Daniel all day." He followed her, unsure of what to say or do. Was he callous to be hungry when his father and brother were injured?

"Your sister and mother took turns too. At least I feel I'm being useful when I'm keeping Daniel entertained. Now, tell me about capturing Tyson."

He explained as they descended the stairs and walked toward the kitchen. "I didn't know Pa was hit until we started home."

"Your mother must be torn over where to spend her time. Now that Tyson's threat is removed, her other patients can see her again."

He cupped her elbow to guide her. "She especially loves helping birth babies."

They entered the kitchen and took seats at the table. Seldom did the family use the dining room. Even visitors appeared to enjoy the kitchen's warm atmosphere. Mama and Rebecca were already eating.

Emma set a bowl of chili in front of Nettie and then him. "We didn't know when you'd come down."

Nettie flicked her napkin across her lap. "Dallas is with Daniel."

Josh picked up his spoon. "Pa wanted to take a nap. He said you'd slipped him something to make him sleep."

"Laudanum. I suspect the loss of blood and the fact I had to dig out the lead wore him out. He was probably already tired. Poor man has had a lot to deal with lately."

Josh recalled that a few days more than a week ago he'd been celebrating his birthday. "Haven't we all?"

Nettie stared at her food. Hell, he hoped she wasn't going to light into him again. Didn't she ever smile or laugh?

Rebecca nattered on about something to do with new barn kittens. "Do you want one, Nettie?"

His wife looked at him. "Josh and I'll have to discuss it. We can't do anything that Mr. Tall Trees wouldn't like. After all, we're using his home."

His sister stared at him. "By the time they're weaned, don't you think you'll have your own place?"

He sent Rebecca a glare he hoped would shut her up. "I can't say for sure. What was that book you've been reading?"

"*Around the World* by Jules Verne. Lance loaned it to me. So far, I like it."

He sat only half listening to Nettie and Rebecca discuss books. He noted the tautness around his mother's eyes. Not only did she appear worried, but tired enough to drop.

This week had been hard on her. Inaccessible to her patients, worry about Tyson and the damage on the ranch, worry about Daniel, and now Pa. Josh had to face the fact she'd worried about him, too, and his sudden marriage.

He reached across the table and took her hand. "Everything will be all right, Mama. You can count on Nettie and me to help out."

She gave a tired-looking smile. "Don't I know that, son? You've both been a blessing this week. And I know Austin will be up and working after a week or two. I can't help worrying about your brother, though. He's facing a long, hard battle."

"He's strong. You know he's got the McClintock stubborn, too. I don't know how long it will take, but he'll walk again. You wait and see."

Even as he reassured his mother, he wondered himself. He'd never known anyone who'd broken his back, but Doctor Sullivan's diagnosis didn't sound optimistic. Would his younger brother be a prisoner of his own body for the rest of his life?

Chapter Eleven

Nettie awoke with a sense of uncertainty. She realized she and Josh would have to remain at the ranch to help, at least as long as Austin was unable to work—and perhaps longer. Although she admired the family and enjoyed being with the McClintocks, she wanted to return to the little cottage where she and Josh lived. There she would have a sense of normalcy and be able to work on making a success of her marriage.

A cheerful thought occurred to her. Now that Bob Tyson and his cohorts were in jail, she should be able to come and go freely. Perhaps she'd go see Stella today. After being constant companions for all her life, she truly missed the camaraderie she and her sister shared.

Humming a happy tune, she peeked into Daniel's room. Arm in a sling, Austin sat beside his son. Daniel was propped up on pillows and in the process of eating breakfast. That was a great sign. Austin waved away her help.

She flew down the steps to the kitchen. Josh sat at the table with Kathryn and Rebecca. Emma smiled and set a platter of ham and bacon next to a bowl of scrambled eggs. Nettie wondered if Emma ever sat down to eat. As if in answer, the woman took a seat at the table.

"I'm glad I didn't miss breakfast." Nettie passed the basket of biscuits.

Emma smiled at her. "I'd have saved some back for you."

Josh looked at the housekeeper. "Hey, you always told me to be here at meal time or do without."

The older woman appraised him. "Doesn't look to me like you missed any meals. Guess you learned to be on time didn't you?"

Nettie said, "This is the first time I've seen you seated. I wondered if you ever got off your feet."

Fork in hand, Kathryn looked up. "Not often. I don't

know how she keeps going full steam all day."

Emma cut a bite of ham. "Humph, you should talk. Never knew anyone could keep up with you."

Nettie asked, "What's the schedule for today? I saw Austin is with Daniel now. By the way, Daniel was eating well."

Josh snatched another biscuit. "I'm going with Buster today to look at the damaged fence. We want to see if the repair held or the wire has to be replaced."

"I wonder if I could go visit Stella for a short while?"

Kathryn patted her arm. "Of course you can, dear. You don't have to ask."

"I'll be back by noon and can take a turn sitting with Daniel or helping Emma, whichever is needed most."

Josh glanced her way. "How will you get there?"

"I thought I'd walk. It's only a couple of miles, isn't it?"

A frown marred Josh's handsome forehead. "You need to learn to ride. Most places are too far to walk plus it's not safe. There are wild dogs, snakes, all sorts of things to avoid."

Kathryn asked, "Can you drive a buggy?"

"I can drive a wagon. I guess a buggy would be the same."

"Good. I'll tell Shorty to get ours ready. You'll save time and your feet. Then Josh and I won't worry about you."

Nettie almost said her husband would not be worried about her, but she simply smiled and said, "Thank you, Kathryn. You're very generous and considerate."

A few minutes later Nettie was on her way to visit her sister. She arrived earlier than she intended, but Finn would already be at work. Stella must have heard her arrival, for she came to the door.

Stella hugged her. "Nettie, I'm so happy to see you. Does this mean that man has been captured?"

Nettie followed her sister inside. "Yes, Sheriff Yates and some others caught Tyson and two of his friends yesterday. Austin was injured in the process. We'll have to stay at the McClintock's ranch for a while longer."

Her sister's blue-green eyes twinkled. "How is married

life now?"

Nettie sank onto a chair. "Confusing. I followed your instructions and they worked I suppose." Nettie fought to keep back her tears.

Stella's blue-green eyes filled with compassion. "Oh, sister, I'm so sorry. Since the two of you aren't in love, I suppose time will bring you closer. You have to let him know what you expect, too. Has it been the same every time?"

Nettie examined her hands. "Well…you see, that's the only time. I mean, the next night we had to move to the ranch. I just couldn't let Josh have his way with me when his sister was next door and his parents were in his brother's room across the hall."

Stella put her hands on her hips. "And why not?"

She heard the pleading in her voice and it embarrassed her. "What if they heard? What would they think?"

Pointing a finger at her, Stella took two steps closer. "Nettie Sue Clayton McClintock, you are a married woman. For heaven's sake, act like a wife. Believe me, your in-laws would be far more shocked that you're not making love than if they heard you were."

She rose and paced. "Oh, Stella, my entire marriage is a mistake. No matter what I do, I'm confused and unsure."

"You'd better straighten out your mind, sister, or your marriage will be in too much trouble to repair. A man has a right to expect his wife to make love. And you're cheating yourself of the pleasure you would share with Josh."

"I know you're right. Maybe I just needed to hear you say so. I'd made a vow to be strong and stand up for myself, but every time I try I make a mistake."

Stella rose and grasped her by the shoulders. "The original Nettie is pretty amazing. Why don't you forget your vow and just be you? I can't imagine a better sister than the one I've always known."

She took a deep breath. "Okay. I'll go back to being shy, boring me."

"You might be shy, but you've never been boring a day in your life."

With a dismissive wave of her hand, she said, "You

would say that because you're my sister."

"Have you looked into the mirror, sister? You're a beautiful woman. More important, you have a kind and generous nature and sing like an angel. Your compassion is why you were such a good teacher with young children."

"You're nice to say those things." Overcome with remorse, she sobbed into her hands. "Oh, I'm such an idiot. I've really made a mess of my marriage."

"Nothing that can't be remedied. Think how you'd feel if Lance was laid up like Daniel and Papa had been shot. Give Josh the consideration you'd expect."

Nettie dried her tears. "I will. Now tell me what's going on with you and Finn and in town."

After visiting for another hour, Nettie drove back to the ranch. Stella had given her a lot to consider. Would she be able to salvage her marriage?

Chapter Twelve

Josh stood on the porch and watched Nettie drive up. She handled the reins like a beginner. If he'd realized how inexperienced she was as a driver, he would never have let her go alone.

Dang, he should have known she was a beginner. Living in coal towns, she walked everywhere and had no occasion to learn about horses and buggies. He strode down the steps to meet her and helped her from the buggy.

She smiled sweetly at him. "Thank you, husband. I had a lovely visit with Stella."

"Horse give you any trouble?" He held her against him as she skimmed down his body until her feet touched the ground.

"None. Has the doctor been by?"

"You just missed him."

Red hurried to take the reins and drive the buggy to the carriage house.

"Thanks, Red." Josh turned and placed his arm around his wife's waist as they climbed onto the porch.

"How're your father and Daniel?"

He couldn't suppress a grin. "Pa's grumbling so I reckon he's feeling lots better." He sobered. "Daniel still can't move his legs, but the gash on his back is slowly healing."

She stood at the rail looking out over the yard. "I guess it was pretty deep if that's what broke his back."

"Not sure if the rock or the fall did the damage. Probably a combination. I don't understand. Daniel was conscious when I went to him and he told me to chase after the shooter. Thank God, I gave up and came back to him."

She glanced at him. "He's lucky you were so inventive. There's no doubt in my mind you saved his life."

Bitterness tinged his voice. "No, if I'd been more alert, he wouldn't have been injured."

Nettie turned him so they faced. "Oh, Josh, you can't really believe that. You weren't the man lying in wait to shoot two innocent people. You're the one who saved your brother."

His knuckles were white where he gripped the porch rail. "I can't get over the image of him lying there pinned under his horse. I have nightmares about that scene over and over."

She slipped her arm across his back. "You should have sweet dreams about you saving him. He could have died, Josh, if you hadn't been so clever."

He peered out across the ranch yard but his mind saw the image of Daniel trapped under his horse. "He may wish he had. Only twenty and look at him stuck in a bed. What if he never walks again?"

"Don't even think that. You have to be optimistic. He'll know the minute we lose faith in his recovery." She linked her arm with his. "Come into the house now."

Inside the kitchen, they found his mother and Emma at work.

Mama smiled as they entered. "How are Stella and Finn?"

"Wonderful. Stella said to remind you about the Independence Day celebration at the park in town tomorrow."

A surprised expression came over his mother's face. "With all that's happened this week, I'd completely forgotten. I hope you'll both plan to go. I'm sure Dallas and Cenora will be there."

Josh put his arm around his mother's shoulders and gave her a light hug. "What about you, Mama? You need a break. This would be perfect."

Emma turned. "Josh is right. I'll sit with Daniel while the rest of you go to the celebration."

Mama stood motionless as if deep in thought. "I don't know if I could leave Daniel. I could use an afternoon somewhere else but he might feel deserted."

Nettie clasped her hands at her breast. "Since Emma is willing to stay with Daniel, why don't the rest of us go? Having that horrid Tyson in jail gives us a reason to celebrate."

And that was the truth. He was ready for a little fun. The town's Independence Day celebration would be a welcome chance to see friends and let off a little steam.

He slid his arm around his wife's waist. "Nettie's right, we should all go. Staying here won't help Daniel. He'd know we missed the celebration because of him, Mama. Bound to make him feel worse."

"Yes, I hadn't considered that. I wish we could take him."

"You can't mean to load him into a wagon and make him feel like he's in a freak show? Mama, he'd hate that. Please don't even consider doing that to him."

His mother threw up her hands. "You're right. I was only thinking of ways to cheer him but being a spectacle would be worse than being in his room."

Emma patted his mother on the back. "Kathryn, you just leave Daniel to me. I'll make his favorite foods and we'll have our own party. I'll even play cards with him."

The women began making plans for food and what-not, so he went upstairs to talk to his brother.

Later that evening, he and Nettie prepared for bed. They might as well be in separate rooms for all the good sleeping in the same bed did. In fact, having her next to him presented more problems than her in another room.

He stripped out of his clothes and crawled between the sheets. Nettie wore her gown that showed all the assets she wouldn't share. Didn't she know what a tease she was?

After turning on his side with his back to her, he waited. The mattress dipped and she stretched out next to him. Fighting the desire her presence created, he closed his eyes.

"Josh?" She touched his shoulder.

Startled, he turned to his back. "What?"

"I've been thinking again, and I realize I was wrong about our coming together here in your parents' home. If you want to, we can have congress."

He raised on his elbow. "Congress? Can't you even say the words 'making love' when you talk about us?"

"You don't love me, so I thought 'making love' was the wrong term. Sorry if I offended you. I guess that means you're not interested tonight."

He leaned forward to nip at her shoulder. "Honey, a

man my age is always interested."

"Oh. You didn't appear to enjoy making love the other time."

He stared at her. "Why the hell would you say that?"

"You just rolled off of me and went to sleep without a word. I thought you'd talk to me and we'd cuddle until we both went to sleep."

Virgins! Save a simple man. "Aw, Nettie, remember how hard a day I'd had with almost no sleep the night before. I was so tired I couldn't stay awake. Can we try again?"

"If you wish. You said before we could be quiet enough that Rebecca won't hear."

Damn, he had said that. At least the bed was against the outside. He'd have to go easy, though, or the headboard would bang against the wall.

He caressed her satin skin then tugged on the ribbons that tied her gown at her shoulders. "We should get rid of all this extra fabric. Slide this over your head."

She sat up and pulled off the gown. "A-All right. Seems indecent, but you said married people see each other n-naked. Stella said the same thing."

He raised up on his elbow to watch her. "You talked with Stella about us?" If that didn't beat all and made him boiling mad. In spite of his ire, the sight of her body hardened him like a wagon tongue.

She lay with her golden hair spread out on the pillow just as he'd imagined and gazed at him with pleading in her beautiful blue eyes. "I had to talk to someone about the mess our marriage has become."

She blinked and he saw the shine of moisture gathering in her eyes. "Stella told me I've been unreasonable. I'm sorry, Josh. I just didn't know what to do to make things right."

His anger fled. "Then I'm glad you talked to her. We got off to a bad start, but this will make things easier between us. Let me show you how."

"How what?"

"How a man makes love to his wife. We start here." He rained kisses across her face before he claimed her lips.

This time when he probed her mouth, her tongue met

his eagerly. He cupped her breast and she raised her shoulders as if to encourage him. When he broke the kiss to suckle her nipple, she moaned in pleasure.

With her no longer being a virgin, he didn't have to go slowly but he wanted her to enjoy their coupling. Inserting a finger in her velvet folds, he continued to lave her breast. Her breathing increased and he rubbed his thumb across her pleasure nub. She moaned again and grasped his head, shoving him harder against her orb.

Granted she was naïve and untried, but he'd been lucky in one thing—obviously she was a passionate woman. He refused to compare her to his other conquests. They'd been women who knew how to have a good time and did so with whoever suited them. Being the only man to touch Nettie gave him a good feeling.

He moved over her, kneeing her legs apart. She cooperated and he positioned his staff above her opening. As he thrust into her, she raised her hips to meet him. He reclaimed her lips and moved his tongue in time to his thrusts.

She threw her legs around him and met each movement. Sensations increased and he knew he couldn't hold out long.

"Get ready. I'm almost there."

"More, faster."

He sensed her building and claimed her mouth before she could yell. As she called out into his mouth, he reached his peak and spilled into her. Collapsing beside her, he pulled her into his arms.

"That was good." Shock hit him. He'd never had pleasure like he had with her.

She pushed her hair out of her eyes. "Good? I thought it was wonderful."

"Yeah, you're right." Sure, he'd had fun with other women that included laughter and teasing along with repeat performances all night, but he hadn't experienced this…whatever it was. Somehow, making love to his wife was different. He held on to Nettie as if afraid she'd disappear.

She traced her finger on his chest. "So, I did all right?"

"Perfect. Did I do all right?" He knew he had. He'd never had complaints before.

"Perfect, or that's what my vast experience tells me."

He laughed and kissed her temple. "Yeah? I thought you caught on awfully quick."

She punched his arm. "As if you were worried about other men."

He exhaled. "I wonder if Daniel will ever make love to a woman. If he'll ever have a wife or be able to walk."

"He's a nice man who's heartbroken now, but his McClintock stubborn will surface soon. When that happens, I believe he'll walk again."

"McClintock stubborn? Thanks a lot, but I hope you're right. Kills me to watch him lying in bed wearing a hopeless expression."

"I hope he truly won't mind if we go to the celebration without him."

"Naw, he'll be sorry he has to miss the day but he won't hold going against us."

"Then let's go to sleep so we'll be able to enjoy tomorrow."

He still cradled her, but he couldn't fall asleep right away. His mind whirled. Who would have thought he would enjoy trying to please his wife? But he had questions about his past and present. He suspected he'd been a fool in many respects.

Chapter Thirteen

Nettie smoothed her pink skirt and adjusted her straw bonnet as the buggy arrived in town. Excitement filled her at the prospect of the first Independence Day celebration in her new home. She and Kathryn had packed enough food for ten people instead of the five going.

McClintock Falls Park was near the center of town. Red and blue banners draped a bandstand in the center and a band was playing when the McClintocks arrived. Nettie scanned the people already there looking for her parents, Stella and Finn, and Cenora and Dallas.

Austin stopped the buggy under a tree and hopped down. "I'll move the horses after we unload. Looks like we have enough for half the town."

Kathryn smiled at him. "We'll see if there's food left to take home."

Arm in a sling, he still tried to help his wife out of the buggy. "Ha, of course there won't be. Everyone knows you're a great cook."

Rebecca hopped down by herself. "I'm going to look for Maddie."

"Stay in sight, please." Kathryn called as the teen raced off.

Josh helped Nettie down and spoke quietly, "Avoid Avis Dunhill's food. Woman is a terrible cook."

She picked up a couple of blankets. "How will I know?"

He carried a basket of food. "I'll show you. She always brings the same things. Even flies avoid them."

Walking beside him, she wrinkled her nose. "Now I'll have to try something of hers out of curiosity."

He claimed a spot and set down his load. "You've heard that 'curiosity killed the cat'. Well, this is one of those instances."

Nettie spread the blankets. Josh went back for the other basket of food.

Kathryn spread a tablecloth in the center of the blankets. "Everyone puts food on those tables at suppertime. Until then, let's leave it here in the shade."

Nettie looked at the large tree canopy above them. "This is a nice spot. We can hear the band. I guess there'll be fireworks as soon as dark arrives."

Kathryn sat gracefully and arranged her skirts. "Oh, yes. Unfortunately, there'll also be speeches. The mayor's are long and dull, but Grandpa's will be short and funny. Sometimes one of the other town leaders also wants to have his say."

"I'm so happy to be here. Thank you for your part in helping my parents. They love living here and Dad enjoys his barbershop. He knows all the gossip." She leaned forward conspiratorially. "Of course, men don't call what they say gossip."

Kathryn laughed and looked at Austin. "Oh, no, of course not. They're just keeping up with the local news."

Austin grinned at his wife. "Glad you understand the difference."

Josh appeared with the largest basket. "My word, Mama, what did you pack? This is heavy as an anvil."

Kathryn held up her hand to stop his comments. "No complaints allowed, son. This is a celebration."

"Okay, I believe I'll stroll around and see who's here. Back in a few minutes." He stuffed his hands in his pockets and walked toward the crowd.

Nettie knew where he was headed. The friends who'd been at his birthday party were gathered around the beer awning. That Isobel Hamilton was there too, hoisting a beer. Nettie's stomach clenched and she fisted her hands.

"Don't pay any attention, dear." Kathryn laid her hand on Nettie's. "You won him and he won't cheat on you."

"I know he won't. He promised to 'forsake all others' and he said he takes that vow seriously. Still, I hate that he still wants to be with the friends who let him drink so much." But she couldn't tear her eyes away from him.

"Let him? I'm sure they encouraged him, mostly because he paid for their drinks as well. I hate that he made those new friends instead of sticking with his old buddies."

"I wonder why he changed."

One of his friends thrust a beer in his hands and another clapped him on the back. Isobel leaned in to flirt with him.

"All his old friends were married or left the area. I guess he felt strange with couples and looked for other single men his age."

Forcing herself to turn away, Nettie shifted position and scanned others at the festivities. "I'm sure my family is here somewhere." She couldn't resist looking back at her husband.

Josh assessed his friends. Somehow they didn't appeal to him as much as they had. He lifted his beer and took a long drink.

He ignored Isobel, but she thrust a piece of paper into his pocket.

Dexter Farris clapped him on the back. "I knew you'd be back with us even though you got leg-shackled. You buying a round?"

"I guess." Josh tossed a few coins on the board that served as a counter.

Wayne Hubbard chortled. "Knew no prissy miss would keep you interested."

Isobel toasted him with her glass. "Let me know when you want to be with a real woman."

Mike Winston punched him on the arm. "Now that Tyson's in jail, reckon you'll leave the woman who trapped you at home and join us in town."

He set down his beer. "Wait just a minute. You're talking about my wife. Show some respect."

Dexter raised his hands. "Whoa, aren't you a little touchy for a man who had a shotgun at his back when he married?"

"I think I've had enough of you and the beer." He turned and strode toward Nettie and his parents.

The nerve of those people. He'd thought they were friends, but now he realized they only wanted someone to buy them drinks and carouse with them. Pa was right, but damned if he'd admit that fact to anyone.

Someone touched his arm. He almost swung but saw Kurt Tomlinson smiling at him. "Glad to see you and your family can join the fun today. Clever of you to help with Tyson's arrest."

"Aw, Sheriff Yates made the plan. Pa got shot, but he's here today. Your wife here with you?"

Kurt gestured to his right. "Yep. We're sitting with her parents today. My folks joined us so we take up a lot of room."

"That's great. I imagine that will happen when Nettie's folks find us. We're expecting Dallas and Cenora and their baby, but they're waiting until the sun's not quite so hot."

"Don't blame them. Babies burn real easy I hear. Say, guess I can tell you even though we haven't told everyone. Dorcas is expecting at Christmas." Kurt beamed bright as the sun.

Josh offered his hand. "Hey, congratulations. That's great news."

Kurt shook and then said, "Well, I was sent to get some lemonade, so I'd better fetch drinks or I'll be in trouble."

"I'll go with you and get some for my folks. Nettie loves lemonade." He thought she did anyway. Suddenly, he wondered why he'd ever drifted away from Kurt's friendship. They'd been best friends since grade school.

Carrying a box of drinks to pass out to his wife and parents, he saw Nettie talking with that Marvin Davis. She leaned back and laughed aloud. He'd never seen her in an out and out guffaw like that. She'd sure never laughed like that with him.

As he approached, Marvin nodded and walked away. When Josh reached his family, he handed out lemonade.

He sat on the blanket, careful not to spill his drink. "What did Marvin want?"

Nettie sipped and glanced at him. "Just to say hello. Thanks for the lemonade. Sure tastes good."

His mother said, "I'm glad you thought of this. I brought milk and cider for supper but not enough to sip on all afternoon."

Nettie gestured toward the bandstand. "Oh, look. Becky

and Lance are in the three-legged race."

Grace and Council Clayton sauntered their way. Council carried a large basket and Grace held a blanket.

Grace asked, "May we join you?"

Austin scooted over. "Of course. We tried to save room for you folks and for Cenora and Dallas. How's the shave and haircut business, Council?"

"Picking up. Have quite a few daily customers who want me to shave them." He peered around. "Getting crowded now, isn't it?"

Josh tuned out the chatter. He couldn't stop thinking about how happy Nettie had looked laughing with Marvin Davis. What had the other man said to cause her reaction? Why didn't she act like that for him?

Had he ever given her reason to? Thinking back, he couldn't think of anything he'd said except just what was necessary. Right then he decided he'd court his wife. Sounded stupid even to him, but he wanted to make her laugh, to bring her joy. What the hell was wrong with him?

***

Nettie leaned back on her hands and enjoyed the day. How lovely to sit with her new family and her parents. Band music drifted over the crowd. Cheers emanated from the games and races being held.

Rebecca and Lance raced toward them.

Lance said, "We won the three-legged race."

Rebecca held up a blue ribbon. "We only got one prize but Lance said I can keep it."

She handed the ribbon to her mother. "We want to enter something else."

With that, she and Lance raced back toward the games.

Her mother said, "Oh, to have that energy."

Kathryn nodded, watching the youngsters run. "Isn't that the truth? Even with all these people around, I think I could fall asleep right here."

Mama reached over to touch Kathryn's hand. "I'm so sorry to hear all you've gone through this week. I'll be out to help sit with Daniel or help Emma while you sit with him."

Her mother-in-law smiled at her then turned to Grace.

"Nettie has been a godsend. I don't know how I'd have managed without her."

The compliment pleased Nettie and warmed her inside. "You'd have managed, Kathryn. You're so efficient."

Josh stood and extended his hand to her. "Let's stroll around and see who else is here, shall we?"

Surprised, she rose. "That sounds nice."

They sauntered between blankets and others strolling the grounds. When they came to a couple seated, Josh stopped.

"Hey, Travis, nice to see you. Louella, Travis, this is my wife Nettie." He turned to her. "Louella and Travis Gibson are good friends I've known most of my life."

Louella scooted closer to her husband. "Won't you sit a while?"

They joined the other couple.

Travis said, "Congratulations are in order, Josh." He nodded at Nettie. "Best wishes. You married a fine man."

Louella asked, "How did you two meet?"

Nettie looked at him but he only smiled. "Josh came to help Finn when he was in Lignite, where my family lived. I thought Josh was the most handsome and charming man I'd ever met." She hated to admit her true feelings, but maybe the others would think she exaggerated.

Louella laughed. "No, no, he can only be the second most handsome and charming man, after Travis."

Travis leaned toward Josh and said, "They must need new dresses."

Nettie blushed. She certainly did need more clothes, but she didn't want her husband to think she was hinting or trying to manipulate him. Fortunately, his response was to wink at her.

She smiled at him. This was turning out to be the most wonderful day since she'd moved here.

Louella clapped her hands together. "Nettie, we'll have to get together and have a party to get better acquainted."

Travis leaned back on his hands. "Yeah, that would be fun. What do you say, Josh?"

"Sounds good to me. We could ask Kurt and Dorcas and Dallas and Cenora and Nettie's sister Stella and her husband Finn O'Neill."

Travis sat forward. "Let's make it happen. How about next Friday at our place at six?"

"Sure. I'll tell Dallas and Finn. Can you talk to Kurt?"

"We'll see you on Friday."

Nettie stood. "We'll look forward to then. What shall I bring?"

Louella appeared to consider. "How about a cake?"

They exchanged goodbyes and walked on their way. Nettie couldn't help being excited.

"They were nice. And our first party as a couple."

Josh linked his fingers with hers. "They are nice. Don't know her very well, but Travis has been a friend since I was six."

"Oh, so I'll have to ask him about your secrets."

"Unfortunately, all my sins are public and my parents will share them if asked. In fact, I'm surprised they haven't regaled you with my exploits."

"Such as?"

"Well, how about the time Kurt, Travis, and I stole mother's sheets and made a tent. We did a pretty good job. Ruined the sheets, of course, where the stakes were. Whew, I can still feel that whipping from that one."

"Oh, my, I can't imagine Kathryn angry enough to whip you."

"Imagine it, but it was Pa that did the whipping. He said I'd made Mama sad and that just wouldn't do. Besides, he said I couldn't take other people's things without permission."

"Guess you remembered next time you wanted something."

"Nettie, boys have short memories about such. I've been in more scrapes than you can imagine. Didn't you ever get into trouble?"

"No, just petty things. Stella and I would fight over silly things like whose ribbon was the prettiest. Or who took up the most of the bed or pulled the covers. I did fight with a girl at school once, though."

"You in a fight?"

"Oh, she was a terrible bully. She stole my favorite

book and wouldn't return it. I saw red and launched myself at her before I remembered she was bigger than me by twenty pounds."

"Did you get slaughtered?"

"No, I was so mad I made her cry and then I jerked back my book and ran home. After that she never bothered me again."

"I've seen you mad and it's a scary sight. I hope you don't get mad at me again."

She wanted to tell him to stay away from Isobel Hamilton if he didn't want to see her angry but she didn't want to say anything that would spoil this day. "Ha, I can bet you're trembling in your boots."

"I am, totally shivering in fear." He slipped his arm around her waist as they walked.

One of the men that had been drinking with Josh at the birthday party walked up. "Well, look at this."

"Hello again, Wayne."

The man named Wayne wore a disgusted expression. "I figured by now you'd be crosswise and fighting. What's happened to you, Josh? Damned if seeing you all cozy doesn't strike me with fear."

Instead of taking offense, she and Josh looked at one another and burst out laughing. With the man staring agape, they walked away.

Nettie nodded toward the long tables set up near the bandstand. "Look, people are putting out their food. You promised to show me Mrs. Dunhill's dishes."

"Don't say I didn't warn you. I'd better go carry Mama's baskets to the tables. I hope she saved back some just for us." He walked faster.

She skipped to keep up. "She did. We packed one basket for us and the big one to put out with the other food. She's a generous person and worried that some might not have much to bring."

"Good news." He helped her sit beside her mother. "You wait with our folks and I'll carry the big basket to set stuff out for others."

Nettie sat in a golden glow of her own as the sun sank

on the horizon. Rebecca and Lance joined them. Dallas and Cenora and baby Houston did too. Even Victor and Zarelda McClintock appeared. Zarelda, or Gran as she preferred, had a canvas chair to sit in and so did her husband.

Grandpa McClintock set up the chairs. "Old bones don't take to the ground too well. Oh, I can sit down all right, but then don't know if I could get up again."

Gran harrumphed and sat down. "We brought food and put it on the tables. I guess you hoarded some over here as usual, Kathryn."

Without batting an eye, Kathryn said, "Yes, I did. Shall I fix you a plate?"

Gran peered toward the basket. "You have fried chicken? And did you bring that chocolate cake I like?"

Josh reappeared and winked at Nettie. "How are you feeling, Gran? Do you need Mama to doctor anything?"

His grandmother sneered. "I certainly do not. Doctor Sullivan takes care of any complaints I have."

"I think Mama brought her doctoring bag just in case, so let us know if I need to fetch the valise from the buggy."

Gran took the plate from Kathryn without a thank you. "Joshua McClintock, you are not as clever as you think you are. You'd do well to respect your elders."

"Now, Zarelda, Josh is just having fun. Be a good sport, won't you?" Grandpa accepted a plate from Kathryn. "My, look at this mouthwatering feast. Kathryn, you outdid yourself."

Nettie served her own plate and dug into fried chicken, potato salad, beet pickles, spiced peaches, deviled eggs, and black-eyed peas. She was glad she'd only had a light lunch because she hadn't tried all of the food Kathryn packed. Her mother had brought a ham and she'd have to eat some of that or hurt her mother's feelings.

Stella and Finn rushed up at the same time as Cenora, Dallas, and baby Houston.

Stella said, "We had trouble finding you."

Cenora sat Houston on the blanket and spread a quilt then moved the baby to her covering. "He may spit up or wet his pants so I don't want him on someone else's blanket."

The chubby baby clapped his hands and laughed.

Finn said, "I'll go put some of our food out."

Josh called, "Hey, bring Nettie a sample of Avis Dunhill's food, would you?"

Finn stopped in his tracks and sent Josh a puzzled glance. "Why?"

Her husband nodded toward her. "She's curious to try Avis's dishes."

Dallas stared at her. "I can understand why since you're married to Josh that you have some kind of death wish, right?"

Josh pretended to be offended. "Ha, ha."

"After Josh's warnings I simply want to see what the poor woman's food is like. She couldn't be as bad a cook as he indicated."

Dallas raised an eyebrow. "Yes, she can. But you'll see for yourself."

Finn soon returned with a plate of food, his basket, and his family trailing him. She accepted the plate and sampled a bite.

She gulped and wished she could spit out the food. "Euww. You were certainly right about the meat. I'll try a bite of cake." She tasted a small morsel.

She spat the bite into her hand and tossed it onto the grass. "Oh, my stars. This sawdust should be labeled as poison."

Her husband smirked. "Didn't I warn you?"

Nettie hadn't been around Finn's parents much but she liked what she'd seen. His mother was shy, but his father talked enough to make up for her quietness. His brother Mac and sister-in-law Vourneen appeared uncomfortable as they set their baby Sean on a blanket.

Nettie smiled at them. "How nice to have you here, too. We wondered where you were. Josh and I walked around but didn't find you."

Finn's mother, Aoiffe, said, "We had a late start. Vourneen was casting up her toes and we weren't sure the poor dear could stand the heat earlier."

Kathryn asked, "Should I get you tea, Vourneen?"

"I could have used something this morning, but I'm fine

now. I think I'm expecting again, you see." She didn't look happy at the prospect.

"Are your parents here, Vourneen?" Nettie asked.

The girl shrugged, a petulant expression on her face. "Somewhere. We gave up looking for them. I just don't feel well enough to traipse around any longer lugging the baby."

Mac scowled at her. "Didn't I ask if you wanted me to carry Sean? What were you thinking to say no?"

Brendan O'Neill, Finn's father, sent what appeared an uncomfortable glance at his youngest son and daughter-in-law and rubbed his hands together. "Weel now, isn't this a lovely gathering? 'Tis looking forward to the fireworks I am."

Austin said, "We've already started eating, but we could do with a blessing, Brendan. Have you one ready?"

Brendan laughed. "Ah, you know 'tis always ready I am. How about this one: May you always have these blessings—a soft breeze when the summer comes," He turned his face into the gentle wind and lifted his hands, "A warm fireside in winter, and always—the warm soft smile o' a friend."

Everyone in their group clapped.

Nettie had heard about Brendan O'Neill's garrulous nature and handy blessings, but this was her first experience in close contact with him at a meal. How could such a cheerful man have a grim son like Mac? At least Finn was fun as well as a good husband to Stella and a hard worker on his ranch next to that of Dallas and Cenora. Finn had certainly proven himself to be clever at solving mysteries in Lignite.

Seeking to draw Vourneen into a more pleasant conversation, Nettie asked, "How old is Sean?"

Vourneen perked up slightly. "He's almost four months. He can't sit up yet, but he can turn over."

Nettie offered her finger for Sean to clasp. "He's a precious child. I know you must be so proud of him."

Vourneen, who couldn't be much older than Lance, glanced dispassionately at her son. "I hope our next is a girl."

Nettie tickled the baby's stomach and was rewarded with kicking and arm waving amid bubble blowing laughs. "How nice that he and his cousin are so close in age. They'll be great friends."

Josh drew her to him. "Fireworks are about to begin. First we have to listen to the mayor and then Grandpa."

Grandpa slowly rose to his feet and spoke louder than he intended, "My remarks will be short but you know the mayor. Man never used one word when a hundred would do."

Everyone within hearing laughed. Soon the speeches had ended and fireworks began. Nettie leaned back and watched the starbursts explode in the sky. That's how she'd felt last night when her husband had made love to her. And this time he'd talked and held her afterward.

Maybe there was hope for her marriage after all.

Chapter Fourteen

On Monday afternoon, Nettie prepared for her first riding lesson.

Josh handed her an apple. "Your horse's name is Zeus and he's a chestnut gelding. Give him the apple and then pet his nose and neck. Let him get used to you."

She was surprised at the softness of the horse's nose. She smoothed her hand along his neck.

Josh adjusted the stirrups. "I hope you can use a western saddle."

"Saddles in Texas are different from those in England. Since I've never used either one, I don't suppose the type matters."

She looked down at her clothes. "Kathryn loaned me this split skirt so I could ride astride. She said side saddles are too dangerous out here."

He helped her mount the beautiful chestnut. "That they are. A woman's leg can be wedged in the curve and hold her prisoner even if she slides off the saddle and dangles. Broken hips, broken backs, snapped necks, and other injuries result."

She held the reins with one hand and the pommel with the other. "I like this split skirt. No petticoats and far more ease of movement."

"First, let go of the pommel and use both hands on the reins. Direct Zeus slowly around the corral. Don't be nervous or he'll pick up on that. Guide him with your knees and the reins, but don't jerk on the reins and hurt his mouth."

So many instructions to obey at once. She looked at the ground. "I'm really high. I hope I don't fall."

"Forget that and concentrate on the horse and your movements. Sit straight. Keep your hands just above his neck. Remember that each of your movements conveys a message to Zeus."

She rode in a slow circle around the corral. "I love

this."

"You're doing well. When you're ready, you can pick up the pace."

She clicked her teeth to increase the speed. Suddenly, she shot sideways. "Oh, no, I'm falling."

Hitting the ground knocked the air from her lungs. Temporarily stunned, she lay looking up at the bright blue sky dotted with a few cotton-like clouds.

Josh bent over her. "Are you hurt?"

She sat up. "Only my dignity, although my bum will probably be sore tomorrow."

He helped her to her feet. "Your bum?"

She stopped brushing dust off her clothes to point at her posterior. "English term, I suppose."

"We say 'bum steer' for bad advice or 'bum' for someone who has no job and isn't looking to change that."

Feeling awkward and foolish, she peered up at him. "Are we through for the day?"

"Always get back on a horse after you fall. Keeps you from being afraid."

She stared at Zeus. The horse stared back with what she thought was a malevolent expression. "But I am afraid."

Josh shook his head. "Doesn't matter, you have to get back in the saddle."

"You're sure?" The horse appeared to have grown in a few minutes. In her mind he looked as tall as the famed Trojan horse must have been,

"Positive. Come on, I'll give you a leg up."

With his help, she climbed onto the saddle. Gradually, her fear dissipated and she enjoyed the horse's movements.

After a half hour of instruction, he asked, "Are you ready for us to head out on the range? I want to teach you to shoot."

"Yes. Let's go." Was she really ready? No, but she wanted to master riding and practice was the only way to do so. And a gun?

Josh opened the gate and grasped Zeus's bridle. With her on Zeus's back and Josh leading him, they walked to where Spartan was saddled and waiting. Josh mounted his horse and they set out slowly toward the range.

"Hold back on speed until you've more experience. You're doing well, though."

She was afraid to look at him for fear she'd lose focus and make a mistake. Even so, she was having a wonderful time. "I'm so glad you're helping me. I never guessed I'd love riding so much."

He grinned. "Oh yeah? Wait until we get back to the barn and I show you how to brush him down and clean his hooves."

"I won't mind, Josh. I know any animal this large requires a lot of care and feed."

He leaned forward to pat Spartan's neck. "Horses are smart and sensitive. Treated well, they're loyal for life. Even some that are mistreated still bond with their owner and forgive."

"I wouldn't want to do anything harmful to this or any horse. Since I don't know anything about their care, I"ll have to depend on you to show me."

He flashed his roguish grin, his blue eyes twinkling with mischief. "Ah, an unsuspecting sucker…I mean worker. What I've always wanted."

She returned his smile. "Hmm, I think I'll check with Kathryn when we go inside to see if I've been hoodwinked."

They rode slowly across the range and she reveled in the experience. Having Josh with her made the time even more pleasant. He pointed out boundaries and named trees and plants she asked him to identify. He might appear an unconcerned rogue, but he knew the ranch and everything included. Hearing the pride in his voice made his love for the land obvious.

"Okay, let's tie our horses here and do some target practice." He tied Spartan's reins to a fence post.

"You're sure? I've never even held a gun." She dismounted. Her legs were like rubber. When she'd recovered, she tied Zeus's reins at the next fence post. Both horses had enough freedom to graze.

"You won't be living in town now. You need to be able to defend yourself. See that log just this side of the trees?"

"Yes. Must have been a large tree before it fell."

"That's your target. See where the limb sticks straight up?"

She shaded her eyes with her hand. "I do but that's not a very wide target."

"It'll do." He took a gun from his waistband. "This is a revolver, called that because this part of the gun revolves as bullets are fed in or fired." He emptied the chambers and handed her the gun.

"What do I do?"

He held out the bullets. "You put these in. I'll do the first one and then you do the others. Most people leave one space empty so the gun doesn't accidentally fire and shoot them. For practice, though, feed in all the bullets."

He stood behind her and held her arms. "Now, sight down the barrel and pull the trigger. Hold the gun with both hands and remain steady. Ready?"

In answer, she pulled the trigger. Nothing moved except a flock of sparrows from the group of trees. "I missed."

"Did you keep your eyes open?"

"Mostly."

He chuckled. "This time, be calm. Think as if you were the bullet and imagine where you'd go. Point at the branch."

She fired again and hit the main tree. "At least I got closer."

They practiced until she hit the branch several times in a row.

"Good, now the rifle." He reloaded the revolver before he returned the gun to his waistband. "Always reload so you're ready for the next emergency.

He pulled his rifle from the saddle scabbard. "This has a kick, so you have to be prepared. Otherwise, you'll get a nasty bruise and land on your um, *bum* again."

He helped her hold the rifle correctly. "Sight along the barrel. This shot travels much further than a revolver bullet, so never fire unless you know what's beyond your line of vision."

She took a deep breath. "Okay, I'm ready. Don't let me fall."

His arms were around her guiding her. She sighted the tree and pulled the trigger. The blast almost deafened her and she fell backward into Josh.

"Good heavens, how do you not go deaf?"

He chuckled. "You hit the tree. Try again."

"There aren't any cows in that pasture behind the trees, are there?"

"Not today. No people either if they followed orders."

Reluctantly, she raised the rifle and took aim. "I can't believe I'm doing this, but here goes." She fired and the branch disappeared, but she fell against Josh again.

Triumph soared through her. "I hit the branch."

"You literally blew the thing away." He turned her to face him. "You sure you've never shot a gun before?"

"Positive. I've played darts and shot a slingshot."

He raised his eyebrows. "I'll bet you're good with those too."

She put her hand on his chest. "Josh, I'm not seeking false praise. Please tell me how I really fared."

He captured her hand. "I'm honest, Nettie. You have an uncanny eye for target practice. Let's hope you're as accurate if someone is shooting back at you."

Dread filled her at the thought and her stomach clenched. "No, let's hope we never find out about that."

He returned the rifle to its place and they mounted their horses.

She turned her mount to ride beside Josh. "I'm amazed Zeus and Spartan didn't jump or try to run away."

"Dallas and I trained them to tolerate gunfire. Important on a ranch."

After an hour, they arrived back at the barn. When she dismounted, her legs refused to support her. She held on to the pommel or she would have fallen. He came to her side and helped her to a bench.

"Takes a while to get your legs under you. When you've more experience, you won't have that problem."

At least he indicated she'd become a better rider and that there would be future lessons. After she rested a moment, they stored the saddles and tack then fed, watered and brushed the horses. She was doing fine until Josh showed her how to clean the hooves with a pick.

"Lean into him and grab his hoof. While you have it up, use the pick to clean out any pebbles that might cause a sore."

Frightened to maneuver such a large animal, she timidly tried to lift his hoof. He whinnied and pushed her aside. She fell on her bum and rolled away from the horse's powerful hooves.

"He knew you were afraid. You're lucky he didn't kick you. Be assertive." Josh demonstrated.

"I'll try again." She was still frightened. Zeus was so large, but she was determined to learn to do all the jobs connected with riding. "If other women can do this, so can I."

"That's the spirit. You'll be an expert in no time."

She doubted that. As much as she'd enjoyed riding with Josh, she so wanted to be able to ride alone. She could visit her mother or sister whenever she pleased if she learned to saddle, ride, and care for a horse.

"Do you always take care of Spartan or do some of the ranch hands help out?"

"I prefer to see after him myself, but Shorty checks on them every evening. Chuck sees to the horses every morning. He makes sure Spartan has hay and water if I haven't done so."

"Good to have back up, isn't it? Like last week when so many bad things happened."

"Yeah. Hope we're through with catastrophes but life is bound to throw up more obstacles. That's just the way things are."

She released Zeus's leg, stood back, and then jumped up and down. "I did it, I cleaned his hoof."

"Move to the other side and repeat the process. Remember to be confident."

"I hope I appear so to Zeus. Inside I'm shaking. He acts like a good horse, though."

"One of the most gentle. Dallas trained him. In fact, Dallas trains all our horses. He has a magic gift."

Bracing herself, she leaned in and lifted Zeus's hoof. "Finn's in partnership with your cousin now. Of course, your grandfather made that possible."

"Finn saved my father's and Dallas's lives last year when we went after rustlers. Your brother-in-law is a crack shot."

She noticed that Josh had done one of Zeus's hooves and all of Spartan's while she still had one to go. "That rascal never mentioned that. He's quiet and kind, but Papa said Finn can defend himself well in a fistfight. I'm glad he and Stella are married and have such a nice place to live."

"Gonna take a lot of work to bring the Tyson place back. There's a big house and several barns and outbuildings. Each one needs paint and repair."

"Could we ride over there sometime and look over the house?"

He shrugged. "Sure, how about tomorrow?"

"If your mother doesn't need me, I'd love that. How long would we be gone?"

"Not much longer than you rode today. Soon we'll put in gates to link the two places, but now we'll have to ride around by the road. Probably thirty minutes over and that much back plus whatever time we spend there. Three hours would be more than enough time."

She finished the last hoof and wasn't sorry to see the end of that chore. "I'll ask Kathryn as soon as I see her. She's probably sitting with Daniel now."

Catching a whiff of herself, she grimaced. "I smell like a horse." She brushed at horsehair and dirt on her skirt. "And look at me. I'd better figure out how to clean this skirt before your mother sees me."

"She won't be surprised. You forget, she rides with Pa and gets just as dirty and sweaty as you have, well, minus falling off her horse."

"Thanks for the reminder." Nettie punched his arm lightly. "But I can't imagine Kathryn ever smelling like I do right now. She's always so elegant."

"She'd think that was funny. I'll tell her you said so."

"You probably will, too." She linked her arm with his. "Come on, let's go to the house. Supper should be ready soon and I'm starving."

Inside the house, Austin awaited them. "Son, tomorrow you need to see that gates are placed here," he pointed to a sketch he'd drawn, "here, and here. Then we can move cattle between our existing ranch and the new purchase."

"I'd planned to show Nettie the Tyson place tomorrow."

Austin shook his head. "That can wait a day or two. First we need to brand the new cattle and get those gates in place. Sorry, Nettie, but business comes first."

She said, "I'm sure there's plenty around here I can do to help out Kathryn and Emma."

Josh grimaced. "You're right, Pa. The boys and I will get started on the gates first thing tomorrow. When those are up and secure, we'll brand the new stock."

"Good. There are unbranded calves over there and I don't want to lose them."

Disappointed as she was, Nettie couldn't begrudge protecting the ranch that fed her and her husband and his family. A place this large required constant improvement and monitoring. The ranch was almost like a small town. They even had a small ranch store where Austin sold things at his cost that cowboys might need on a day to day basis.

Chapter Fifteen

Josh tightened the last screw. "Give it a try now."

Chuck opened then closed and locked the gate. "Works fine. That's all three set in place and just at quitting time."

Josh picked up his tools and stuffed them in his saddle bag. "Right, time to head back."

They rode back to the barn. Tonight, Josh and Nettie would be visiting Kurt and Dorcas Tomlinson. After a hard day, he looked forward to the occasion. He readied the small buggy and harnessed Poseidon.

"Shorty, in about twenty minutes, would you bring the buggy to the house?"

"Sure will."

He removed his shirt and dunked under the pump at the horse trough. Using his soiled shirt to dry off, he walked bare-chested to the house. His mother would scald his ears if she saw him, but he didn't have a clean shirt with him.

Sure enough, she was in the kitchen when he came through. "Going native, son?"

Deflecting her sarcasm, he asked, "Nettie tell you we're going to a party at Louella and Travis's place tonight?"

Mama nodded. "She did and I'm glad you two are visiting with other couples your age. I'm sure you'll have a good time."

"Nettie's supposed to bring a cake."

Emma pointed to a box covered with a towel. "She made one. In fact, she made two so we could have one here tonight."

"See you in a bit." He took the stairs two at a time. In his room, Nettie stood before the washstand mirror.

"I'm ready." Her gaze locked with his in the mirror. "I'm nervous."

"No need. You've met some of the people who'll be there. I imagine Dallas and Cenora will come. Probably Kurt and Dorcas Tomlinson as well. Your sister and Finn should help you relax. Anyway, you'll be among friends."

She turned, her hand at her rib cage. "I'm really happy to be going to a party or dinner. I'm not sure what you'd call tonight."

He sat on the chair and toed off his work boots. "An occasion."

She wore her blue dress. Darn, he forgot she didn't ask for things and only had a couple of decent dresses. Just the same, she looked regal with her hair piled high on her head and a pair of…wait. "Are those Mama's earbobs?"

She touched her ear lobes. "Aren't they lovely? She said they match my dress and insisted I borrow them. Oh, and Kathryn said we're going to town soon and get fabric to sew me another dress. What color should I buy?"

He stepped out of his dirty denims and pulled on clean ones. "Don't imagine you'll have that much choice at the mercantile. You look real nice, Nettie. Even though I like your hair down, that style is pretty."

"Why, thank you." She beamed so he figured he didn't compliment her enough. Having a wife was sure more complicated than an experienced woman friend.

When he'd pulled on his black, hand-tooled dress boots, he went to the washstand. "Guess I'd better shave again. Too bad we aren't close to your father's barber shop."

Quickly, he lathered his lower face and shaved off the stubble. Then he slicked back his hair. He checked both cheeks and chin and decided he was good enough to go.

"Mrs. McClintock, are you ready for our evening out?" He offered his arm.

"Yes, husband, I am." Smiling, she picked up a shawl and they left the room.

Nettie wanted to gather every sensation and save them. From the buggies outside the Gibsons' small but attractive home, they weren't the first to arrive. Travis opened the door and welcomed them.

Butterflies swarmed in her abdomen, but she forced herself to calm down. She handed the cake she'd brought to Dorcas. "You didn't tell me what kind, so I made apple and raisin with a burnt sugar icing."

"Wonderful." Louella accepted the box holding the dessert. "I think you know Cenora and Dallas and Dorcas and Kurt. Of course, you know your sister and Finn. We have to keep parties small so we can seat everyone."

Nettie sat on the sofa between Cenora and Stella. At least she did know them. Having met the other two women didn't mean she was comfortable with them.

Cenora asked, "How is Daniel?"

"His spirits appear a little better now that he's downstairs and can use the wheelchair to get around."

"Dallas and I are that thankful the lad can move from room to room."

Louella clasped her hands to her chest. "We're praying Daniel will walk again. I know it will be a long recovery, but he's young and strong."

"You left Houston at home?" she asked Cenora.

"My parents came to stay overnight so they could take care o' him. I'm still nervous when he's out o' me sight. With Ma and Da at our place, the baby is in his own bed and rooms he's used to."

Nettie loved hearing Cenora speak because her voice still carried a musical Irish lilt. Dallas rose from the chair at his wife's side to speak with Josh.

Dorcas sat in a chair near the sofa. "I'm glad to get to know you, Nettie. Kurt and Josh have been friends since they were small boys."

"Yes, he told me. We're both pleased we can get together tonight."

Louella clapped her hands. "Friends, let's gather around the table for dinner, and then we can visit and enjoy games."

As they rose, Nettie overheard a man say the name "Isobel" and stiffened. Although she listened, she couldn't discern anymore of the conversation. Josh had been so attentive lately, why did hearing that woman's name upset her so much?

She hated to believe she was the jealous type. Considering the basis for her marriage, she couldn't stop envy where Isobel Hamilton was concerned. After all, that's who Josh had intended to visit when he climbed in her window.

Nettie pasted a cheerful smile on her face and sat where Dorcas directed. She found herself seated at Travis's right and beside Josh and across from Louella.

After the meal, Josh interpreted Dallas's signal to step into the next room.

Grim expression on his face, Dallas handed him a note on familiar pink paper. "What are you going to do about this situation? Woman saw me in town and had the gall to ask me to be her courier."

Josh opened the note, read it, and then crushed it into a ball in his palm. "She keeps sending me these. Slipped me one in front of everyone at the Independence Day celebration."

"Well? You say anything to her?"

Frustrated and angry, Josh shook his head. "I thought she'd get the hint when I ignored them, but she keeps sending the damned things."

"Apparently, Isobel doesn't understand subtle. You'll have to tell her in no uncertain terms she's part of your past."

"Man, if Nettie learns I've talked to Isobel, she'll be so angry I don't know what she'll do. She may look shy, but she has a temper and she hates Isobel."

Dallas sent him a disgusted glance. "Do you blame her?"

"No, but I assured Nettie I would be faithful. If she sees me talking to Isobel, she'll think I lied."

His cousin poked his chest. "You'll have to do something, Josh, or Isobel will manage to cause trouble in your marriage."

Josh started to toss the pink note into the grate, but thought he'd better dispose of the incriminating material elsewhere. He stuffed the crumpled ball into his pocket.

Nettie sat with the women, but she caught the name 'Isobel' from Dallas and Josh's side conversation. She strained to hear what they were saying, but Louella's chatter and laugh drowned out the men's conversation.

Was Josh breaking his word? She spotted Dallas passing a pink piece of paper to Josh and wondered what that represented. She'd been so happy tonight, being included like other couples. That woman's name set her mind whirring with images and thoughts of illicit meetings.

She forced an attentive expression on her face, but the women's talk receded to a murmur as she considered her husband. At the Independence Day celebration, he'd spoken to Isobel. Was he still interested in that woman? Her jealousy was driving her crazy and she had to stop.

***

The next morning after breakfast, Nettie spent time with Daniel while Josh worked around the ranch. He'd taught her to play pinochle and twenty-one.

He dealt the cards for a game of twenty-one. "How's married life?"

Shocked at the question, she had to consider before she answered. "Not exactly what I expected, but we're getting there."

"Sorry you're stuck here, but thanks for helping out. Mama needs someone besides Emma to talk to."

"Have you forgotten Becky?"

He looked at the cards. "She's a really nice sister, but she's only fourteen. If Mama were trapped at home with only Becky, Emma, and Pa, she'd go crazy. She's used to being around people and helping them."

"I know she loves healing and is a compassionate woman. Now that Tyson is in jail, your mother had a couple of visitors consult her yesterday."

"Yeah? That's good." His face contorted with pain. "I hate" he gestured at his leg and the room, "this. I may be the one to go crazy."

Nettie's heart ached for the young man. Before she could answer him, Doctor Sullivan appeared at the door. Ahead of him, he pushed a chair with wheels. Behind him, Kathryn and Austin followed.

Austin still wore a sling and Kathryn had convinced him to wait until Monday to resume riding on the range. He'd lost a lot of blood and the bullet had fractured the bone in his upper arm. Even with Kathryn's excellent care, so far Austin hadn't recovered full use of his arm.

"Looks as if my patient is becoming a card shark. How are you this morning, Daniel?"

Daniel turned his cards face down. "You'll have to tell me, Doc."

Nettie waited in the hall while the physician examined Daniel. Soon, the doctor called her back into the room.

Doc Sullivan tapped the wheelchair as he faced Daniel. "This is what we used to call a Bath Chair because they were so popular in Bath, England and elsewhere that people came to take mineral and hot spring baths. I just call this a wheelchair. Since you have good upper body strength, this will allow you to get around rather than remaining stuck in this room."

Austin touched his son's arm. "We're preparing you a room downstairs. Then, you can move around the main part of the house as you wish."

Daniel looked at the wall. "I *wish* to walk, not lay in bed or sit in that damned chair like I was ninety."

Nettie wanted to reassure him, but thought that better left to his parents and for her to keep her counsel while they were in the room.

Kathryn stood at the foot of his bed. "You will walk again, Daniel. Just give yourself time to heal. In the meantime, the wheelchair will offer you a little freedom."

He looked at the doctor. "I don't mean to seem ungrateful, but—"

"Just give it a try." Doctor Sullivan pushed the chair near the bed. "Consider this chair another part of your recovery."

"You think I'm going to stand up and walk over to sit in that contraption?"

"No, you'll need to have help getting into and out of the chair. Austin, I don't think we need to put pressure on you yet, but Nettie and I can help now."

The physician directed her to assist on Daniel's right side while he lifted from the left. She climbed onto the mattress with her knees and wedged her shoulder into Daniel's armpit. Her brother-in-law slung his arms around their shoulders. Slowly, they scooted the young man toward the bed's edge and she swung her feet to the floor ready to stand.

Doctor Sullivan said, "All together now on three. One, two, three-e-e."

Slowly, they lifted Daniel onto the chair. The physician adjusted her brother-in-law's legs and feet on the footrest. His broken leg clunked against the wood.

"There's no cushion for his back." Kathryn nibbled on her bottom lip.

"He has to lean back or he could fall forward onto the floor. Of course, if this is too uncomfortable, Daniel, we can belt you in. You can fold a blanket to pad the back and seat, but take care."

"I can't control my legs but, by golly, I can move my arms." He rolled the chair a few inches forward and then back."

"And the exercise of moving the chair will be good for your overall health. Kathryn, you can agree with me, can't you?"

"Of course. Lying in bed is necessary for recovery, but too much leaves the patient weak and his muscles atrophy."

At the last word, alarm spread on Daniel's face. "Mama, you've been massaging my good leg and feet a couple of times a day. You said that would help prevent deterioration."

The doctor nodded. "But this is the next stage, Daniel. I have faith in your recovery if you follow the plan your mother and I have laid out. I'm not saying life will be easy for the near future, but you can't give up or you'll be stuck in that bed forever."

Daniel's face took on a fierce expression. "No, I won't give up. I'm going to walk again or die trying."

Austin grabbed his hand. "Don't put it that way, son. Leave it that you're going to walk again. I know you can, but you have to allow time for healing."

After the doctor left, Daniel looked at each of the other three people remaining in his room. "You think we could hire a man to help me out?"

He nodded at Nettie. "I really appreciate all you've done to help, Nettie, but sometimes I'm too embarrassed to ask you to help with…personal functions."

Kathryn said, "Of course, I should have thought of that."

Nettie met Daniel's gaze. "I don't know anyone your

age who'd be free to spend the day, but Lance would help. I'm just not sure he's strong enough to help you in and out of the chair by himself."

She explained to Austin and Kathryn, "He wants to be a doctor someday if he and my parents can save enough money to send him to a university. He's running errands at the mercantile and doing anything else he can find to earn a little cash, but I believe he'd enjoy helping."

Nodding slowly, Daniel brightened. "Lance is someone I could tolerate on a daily basis. Doesn't talk too much, has a good sense of humor, and is intelligent."

Austin laid his hand on his son's shoulder. "Great. I'll send a note to the Claytons and ask them out for a visit. We can talk about what you need and see if Lance is interested."

Nettie stayed with Daniel while his father rested and his mother saw a patient who'd come to the house.

They played cards and then she read to him. When Josh came in, he and she helped Daniel back onto the bed.

Daniel sank onto the pillow. "Who'd think sitting up could be so exhausting? Think I'll take a nap until supper."

Kathryn came into the room. "You two run along and I'll stay with him."

Nettie and Josh retreated to the room they shared.

Chapter Sixteen

"I'm glad you came back early. Daniel was tired but I couldn't help him to bed alone. He's embarrassed for any of the ranch hands to see him like he is and your father isn't quite ready to lift that much yet."

"Damn, but I hate seeing him like that. Thanks for staying with him."

"He's a nice young man and I'm glad he lets me help."

"You want to go for a ride? We can go over and check out the Tyson place."

What she wanted was a nap, but she couldn't pass up a chance to go riding. "I'd like that. Shouldn't you call it the 'new McClintock place' now?"

He tilted his head and grinned. "Guess I should. You coming with me?"

"Let me change into your mom's riding skirt. I'll hurry." She opened the armoire and pulled out the tan skirt she'd brushed clean and a fresh white shirt.

He turned. "I'll saddle the horses and wait for you in the barn."

By the time she changed and told Kathryn where they were going, Josh had led the horses near the back door. She managed to climb into the saddle without his help or using the mounting block.

"Okay, I'm ready. Where is the new McClintock place?"

"We installed the gates this week. We can save time getting there by riding across the range instead of following the road."

Nettie didn't know what the horse's gait Josh chose was called, but she could ride beside him without jarring her bones and even converse with him. In fact, she enjoyed getting out of the house and riding. She appreciated that Josh was making an effort to spend time with her.

She'd been so discouraged about their relationship, but at times like this she hoped they could have a normal marriage. Was she imagining that he was trying? Perhaps he was only placating his parents. No, she determined to follow her own advice for Daniel and to be positive about the future.

They went through one gate and she pointed ahead. "Aren't those mesquite trees? Didn't you tell me they were not good for the range?"

"Right, but we're on the new McClintock place land now. Tyson neglected the place for several years. Ranchers can't afford to do that and keep the pastures clean."

"What will you do?" The trees appeared to be sprouting everywhere.

"We'll try burning some. Small ones we'll cut off. The roots go deep—really deep—so they're hard to kill. They steal water the grass needs. Make good firewood though."

"Looks as if you'll have a lot of kindling."

"Mesquite burns really hot and is great for a barbecue. Gives the meat a nice flavor, but too much will put out too much heat for a fireplace chimney."

"How far are we from the house?"

"Just over that hill you'll be able to see the homestead. Used to be a model ranch. Don't know what caused Tyson to get into drinking and gambling, but like I said, he lost everything."

They rode in silence for a while until they reached the crest of the hill Josh had mentioned. There, they paused and gazed at the lovely valley below. At least, she thought it could be if cared for again.

The large, two-story house faced a tree-lined lane to a larger road that probably went to McClintock Falls. A large barn, equipment shed, what probably was a chicken coop, what might be a pig pen, a paddock, corral, and several other buildings sprawled behind the main home. One building even looked like a small house.

As they rode closer, the neglect became more and more evident. Peeling paint, missing poles in the paddock fence and corral, and other signs showed negligence. They dismounted and tied their horses at the hitching rail.

Nettie surveyed the house. "Ignoring this place was criminal. He must have had men working here who lost their jobs, animals who suffered from inattention."

Josh cupped her elbow and led her up the steps to the front door. "And he lost his wife and children, who moved away to live with his wife's family. But it's ours now and we'll fix it up and make it a thriving ranch again."

She stepped around a missing porch board. "I'm glad. Seeing a house and buildings so dilapidated is sad. When I find a house in this condition, I always have the urge to restore it."

He opened the door. "That's good to hear, Mrs. McClintock. Welcome to your new home." He scooped her into his arms and carried her over the threshold and set her down in the foyer.

She threw her arms around him. "Do you mean we'll be living here?"

"We'll have to make a lot of repairs first and the place needs plenty of soap and water."

Peering around, she was aghast. "How long ago did Mrs. Tyson leave?"

"I'm not sure exactly, but about three or four years ago."

She ran her fingers across a lamp table, revealing a thick layer of dust. "Apparently the home hasn't been cleaned since her departure."

"We can take care of scrubbing later. Let's inventory the contents and check for roof leaks, broken windows, rotted floors, and vandalism."

He pulled a pencil and a folded piece of paper from his pocket. "I'll list what needs immediate attention on one side and less important repairs on the other. Try to overlook the dust and filth and concentrate on the basic structure."

She curtsied. "Lead on, Mr. McClintock."

Among the grime, they found good furniture mixed in with stained and broken pieces. In the parlor, Nettie spotted a treasure, a piano. She raced to the instrument and raised the keyboard cover. Her fingers tapped out what she remembered of a tune.

"Hey, that's good. I know your family members are

musical, but I didn't know you played piano."

"We had to leave ours in England and it broke my heart. Even though it was a family piece, shipping would have been too costly." She sat on the bench and played another song.

"This needs tuning, but it's a wonderful find. I think Papa can tune pianos." Reluctantly, she stood. "Time to move on."

He brushed aside a curtain. "Oops, broken window pane here but someone has boarded over the hole. Water damage from rain though." He made a notation on his list. "We'll have to check each window. Tyson and his buddies must have roughhoused or thrown things in the house."

As they continued, Nettie kept track of rooms. Downstairs there were the foyer, parlor, dining room, mud room, kitchen, pantry, and a bedroom at the back of the house. Upstairs, they found five bedrooms.

Josh checked ceilings then the wall between the master bedroom and the one beside that. "With this roof leak, I'll have a large repair here. I could probably take part of this room and make a bathing room."

"Are you serious? That would be wonderful."

"Pa and I have been talking about putting one in the house and I don't see why we shouldn't have one here as well. We think we've figured out water delivery and drains. Complicated, but we can handle the work."

They moved on to one of the other upstairs rooms. The bed was made neatly and everything appeared in order except for the layer of dust.

"You can certainly tell what Tyson used and what hasn't been used since his wife left." She opened a drawer and found items of clothing still there along with the remains of a mouse nest. After pulling out and tipping the contents upside down, she replaced drawer. "I guess they couldn't take everything when they left. Don't think they wanted that nest."

"You know, this is to be our home now and there's no one here but us. This nice bed is inviting. Don't you agree, wife?"

She whispered, "In the daytime?"

"Why not?" He pulled her into his arms.

His kiss melted any resistance she might have had. Without breaking their embrace, they edged toward the bed. Josh released her to throw the dirt-laden coverlet onto the floor. Doing so created a cloud of dust that set them coughing.

A loud knock came from the front door.

From what sounded like the foyer, a man's voice called, "Hello, McClintock, is that you in there?"

Josh and she locked gazes. He exhaled and strode to the hall. "Up here but I'm coming down."

Josh adjusted his pants as he headed down the stairs. When he reached the foyer, he found a man the size of a smokehouse. Tall himself, Josh figured the man would top his own six feet three by at least five inches. The man's rusty red hair, full beard, and piercing blue eyes gave him a formidable appearance.

The giant stuck out his hand. "Howard Pierson. Most folks call me "Grizzly"."

Josh shook the huge paw and thought the man looked enough like a bear to fit the name. "Josh McClintock. Sorry I didn't get to come when my father met you. My wife and I are inventorying the house for repairs."

Grizzly forked a thumb over his shoulder. "I been living in the little house at the back. I was foreman when there was anything to look out for. I know things is in a bad state, but I wasn't allowed to repair or replace anything."

"You know how many head of cattle there are?"

The big man shook his head. "Over three hundred plus those born since last tally. I was fixing to brand calves when the foreclosure came. Figured the new owner would prefer his own brand."

Josh remembered his father mentioning keeping on a caretaker. "Who's paying you now?"

"Austin McClintock. Your pa gave me some cash to keep vandals away and see nothing was hauled off."

Josh said, "There's a lot of damage in here from broken windows, roof leaks, and such."

Grizzly looked at the stair case. "There was a leak in the roof, but I patched it best I could. Reckon you'll want to get some shingles and make a more sightly repair. Until your pa gave me living expenses, I hadn't been paid in six months. I love this place and just couldn't abandon the ranch and the animals."

"You here by yourself?"

"All but two of the hands left and they only stayed 'cause they were drinking buddies with Bob, that's Bob Tyson. Now they're gone too. Heard they was arrested with Bob."

What Josh could see of his face among the beard took on a troubled expression. "Look, I wasn't a part of all that. Made clear to Bob I was only interested in taking care of the ranch. Austin McClintock said you'd work things out when you took over. I'm sure hoping I still have a job."

Josh pursed his lips fighting for time to make a decision. "You've been here a long time?"

"Started as a cowboy when I was sixteen. Worked my way up to foreman. This was a good ranch until…well, until a few years ago."

"We can work something out. I remember when this was one of the best spreads around. Sure is a shame the place has been allowed to deteriorate so badly."

Grizzly stared at his boots and slowly shook his head. "Hurts me to see the way things are. I haven't had a dime for repairs in over two years. Like I said, six months ago, Bob even ran out of money to pay my salary but said I could stay if I wanted. I figured somebody needed to look after the place. Knew he couldn't hold on to it for long the way things were going."

"You want to show me around the grounds?"

A smile split the big man's face. "Sure would like that."

"Let me tell my wife…oh, here she comes. Nettie, this is Grizzly Pierson.

Eyes wide, she smiled. "Nice to meet you."

Grizzly removed his hat. "Ma'am."

Josh extended his hand to Nettie. "He's about to give me a tour of the buildings. Would you like to come?"

"Sounds interesting." She handed him the pencil and sheet of paper he'd left in the bedroom.

Grizzly led the way. "Let's start with the big barn. Only horse left is mine but there's room for twenty plus a lean-to back of the paddock for a remuda. Used to have six men working here besides me."

After touring the outbuildings, they arrived back at the house.

Josh stood near the horses. "Door was unlocked when we arrived. Pa didn't get a key when he bought the place. You have one?"

Grizzly scratched his beard. "Don't even know where to look. Did you check the drawers on the kitchen?"

Josh said, "No, we were looking for what needed immediate repairs."

"Far as I know, Bob didn't lock the place after Miss Jenny left. He sort of gave up."

Nettie surveyed the grounds. "Sounds like he gave up before then or she'd still be here."

Grizzly held his hat in his hands. "Yes, ma'am. Bob loved her even though he fell into bad habits. After she left, well, he changed even more and fell further into the bottle. That's when he stopped making repairs."

"We'll get a crew over here to clean up the place and start on repairs. You need anything in the meantime, you know where to find me."

The large man gazed fondly at the house. "Can't tell you how glad I am to hear that. I love this old place."

Josh helped Nettie mount Zeus and then climbed onto Spartan. As they rode away, Grizzly turned to go back toward the barn.

"Well, Mrs. McClintock, what do you think of your new home?"

"I love everything but the dirt and neglect. I'll tackle the dirt next time we come. Do you mind if I ask my mother and sister to help clean?"

"Of course not. I figured we'd hire some women from town to help get it livable. Gonna take a lot to get that parlor furniture where you'll be willing to sit on it."

"But most of the pieces are good. I'm excited. I never dreamed I'd ever live in such a luxurious place."

"Well, thanks a lot. You thought I'd have you camping out?"

"No, I thought we'd have to stay in Mr. Tall Trees place until he wanted to return and then we'd rent a place like the one where my family lives. I love their house and would be more than happy to live in a place like that. This will be so much better, though."

"I agree, but that will be a lot to clean. We'll have to hire someone to help you, Nettie. I know you're in good health, but a house that size requires a lot of care. I want you to have time for fun and visiting."

"Thank you, Josh. You'll be awfully busy for a long time. Who'll you get to help you with repairs and then ranch work?"

"Soon as the bunkhouse is in shape, I'll hire some hands. Then they can help repair the rest of the place."

"You're letting Grizzly stay there?"

"Yeah, clearly he loves the place. Hadn't been paid in six months and yet kept looking after things. Guess if it hadn't been for the chickens and garden he wouldn't have had anything to eat."

He glanced at her. "What's your favorite thing about the house?"

Nettie met his eyes. "That we'll have our own home. I hope we can have a good marriage there, Josh. One where we have children and grow old together in happiness."

He smiled at his wife's lack of guile. "My wish too." But he wondered if that would happen.

So many bad things had occurred recently. The sight of Daniel in that wheel chair speared his heart. What if his brother was stuck in that contraption for life? The thought chilled him to the bone.

Stay positive, he remembered his naïve wife's admonition. Damned if he wouldn't try. At least Pa was regaining his strength. Monday, Pa was determined to go back to work on the ranch. That would free Josh to work on the new place.

His own place.

No, his and Nettie's place.

Suddenly he shivered in spite of the bright sun overheard. An itch between his shoulder blades warned him more trouble was sure to come.

Chapter Seventeen

Nettie gushed to Kathryn, "There are five bedrooms upstairs and one down. I think the one on the first floor is intended for a cook or housekeeper. I just never thought I'd live in such a grand place."

"Wonderful that this worked out. Austin and I so wanted to keep our boys nearby. This is a perfect solution for you and Josh."

"You can't imagine how filthy that house is. I'll need to take a lot of cleaning supplies. If you don't have something for me to do here tomorrow, I'd better go to town in the morning and stock up."

"We probably have all the things you'll need. I have a good stash of soap and beeswax and you know where the ragbag is. I'm not trying to talk you out of going into town, Nettie. I just want you to know you're welcome to help yourself to anything we have."

Nettie felt moisture prick her eyes. "You're so kind, Kathryn. I'm so lucky to be in your family."

"We're lucky to have you. I couldn't have picked a better daughter. Now, get washed up for supper. Emma and I have a good meal prepared. Daniel is coming downstairs."

"That's wonderful. I'll hurry and get cleaned up." She ran up the stairs.

Here she'd been focusing on her and Josh's future and for a few hours she'd forgotten about Daniel. Moving downstairs would give him more freedom, but he must be filled with despair. At least with the wheelchair, he could look outside and move from room to room.

Oh, and that meant her parents and Lance were coming. Washing took more time because of the house's grime coating her. She blushed to think of what almost happened in the unused bedroom. How embarrassing if Grizzly had walked in on them making love.

She was buttoning her blue dress when Josh came in. From his wet hair, she knew he'd washed at the pump.

He tossed his shirt onto the floor and grabbed a clean one. "Not sure you want that grimy shirt with the other dirty clothes."

She brushed her hair. "Daniel's moving downstairs tonight."

"So Pa said, and your folks are coming for supper. I hope Lance is interested in helping Daniel."

"I think he will be. Lance wants to become a doctor someday if my folks can save enough for university. Papa used all his savings moving here and taking over the barber shop. That means they have to start over saving for Lance's education." She'd planned to contribute her teaching salary, but now there was no teaching position.

He clasped her waist and met her gaze in the mirror. "Hey, cheer up. We saw our new home, your folks are coming to supper, and we met our first employee." He rested his chin on her shoulder and nibbled her neck. "How about that—we have an employee and we haven't even moved in yet."

She laughed in spite of herself and turned to face him. "You're right. Today's been special already, and looks to be good the rest of the evening."

He brushed his lips across hers. "You're pretty as a picture, wife."

"You're very handsome, husband." She heard the sound of a buggy and team.

He offered his arm. "Time for the perfect couple to go downstairs."

Papa helped Josh get Daniel down the stairs. Lance brought the wheelchair. Austin stood at the foot of the stairs looking as if he could barely resist pitching in. Kathryn stood beside him with her hand on his arm.

They'd just arranged Daniel in his chair when Cenora and Dallas arrived, with him carrying Houston.

When they were all seated, Austin said grace then smiled at those gathered around the table. "We have a lot to be thankful for. Good to have all three of our sons dining with us."

Dallas smiled tenderly at Austin then Kathryn. "Good

of you to include me as a son, even though I'm only your nephew."

Kathryn reached over and touched his cheek. "I don't ever want you to forget your wonderful parents, but you know you're as much my son as if I'd given birth to you."

Nettie's father nodded. "Good to be here as one big family."

She said, "You won't believe what's happened. Josh and I are going to be moving into the former Tyson place, which is now the new McClintock place."

Grace clapped her hands to her heart. "Why, that's great news. What's the house like?"

Josh smiled at Nettie, then her mother. "We went there earlier today and found we have a lot of work to do before we can move in any of our things. Just getting it clean enough to live in will be a major job."

Kathryn nodded at her son. "Soap and elbow grease will remedy that soon enough."

Her mother said, "Now, Kathryn, you're needed here, but I'll be happy to help. I imagine Stella will, too."

Cenora reached out and squeezed Nettie's hand. "Sure, and I'll be helping. Can I bring Houston?"

Nettie shook her head. "Oh, the place is too filthy, Cenora. I'm sure you wouldn't want your baby anywhere near there until the house is cleaned. Josh's and my clothes were unbelievably dirty just from walking through the rooms."

"No matter then. I'll leave him with Ma and Da. They complain they don't see him enough. Sure and I'd like to help you get settled in your new home."

"Thank you. I haven't forgotten how you and Dallas prepared Mr. Tall Trees dwelling for us. It's a lovely cottage." What a lovely couple Cenora and Dallas were. Nettie knew she was lucky to be in this extended family.

Kathryn looked at Daniel then at Austin. "I do feel as if I should remain here. I don't mind paying someone from town to do my share, though."

Josh shook his head. "Mama, you know I have money saved. I can take care of hiring whoever we need. I do want to talk to Pa about ranch hands and cattle, but I'll do that later."

Kathryn turned to her husband. He nodded, as if she'd asked him a question.

Her mother-in-law looked at Lance. "Daniel is downstairs, but he still needs someone to help pass the time by playing games, helping with hygiene, and so forth."

Daniel held up a hand. "I can explain, Mama. Lance, I wondered if you would be willing to be…I guess you'd say be my nurse-helper. Nettie said you're interested in medicine. I have to admit this would mostly be lowly servant duty, but you'd be paid."

Lance, who'd grown six inches in the short time they'd been in town, broke into a wide grin. "Sure, Daniel, I'd like that. Sounds better than running errands and sweeping out a store. What would you want me to do?"

"After supper, let's go into my room and I'll show you. The hardest part would be helping me into and out of this chair."

"I'll try and see if I can manage without hurting you. I'd sure like the job but you'll need to explain exactly what you want me to do."

Conversation took on a light note and continued long after the last bite of dessert had been consumed.

Eventually, Daniel's face grew taut. "Lance, why don't we start now and see if you can help me to bed?"

Dallas stood and said, "Josh and I'll just go along and watch but be handy in case we're needed."

Coming around the table to stand by Daniel, Lance asked, "Shall I push your chair?"

"You can be back up this time. All of a sudden I'm a bit tired but think I can manage."

Austin opened the double doors to the sun room, which now would be Daniel's room.

Daniel set his features and gripped the rims to control the wheels. "We'll see how I navigate through the furniture on my own." He led the way and his brothers and Lance followed.

Nettie and her mother gathered plates and cutlery and each carried a load to the kitchen.

Emma shooed them out. "You two go on and visit. Kathryn insisted I take a nap this afternoon so I'm fresh as a daisy and will have this tidied up in no time."

Nettie leaned toward her mother. "I'd bet good money Kathryn didn't take a nap. She looks ready to drop from exhaustion and worry."

Her mother looked toward her hostess. "I don't wonder, poor dear woman. Too much has happened in such a short time. Thank goodness that man Tyson is in jail."

"Mama, you can't imagine how sad that house is." Nettie held her thumb and forefinger a quarter inch apart. "Dust this thick is everywhere. Liquor and beer bottles litter the rooms he used and there are burn marks and moisture damage on the furniture. A few pieces are even broken, as if someone scuffled and fell."

Her mother hugged her shoulders. "Don't worry, soap and water does wonders, along with beeswax. I'll bring a broom, mop, and buckets with me."

***

The next morning, Nettie loaded cleaning supplies into the wagon and climbed aboard. They hadn't found even a bar of soap at the new house. She wondered if that meant Mr. Tyson had quit bathing. Rebecca carried another load of supplies and climbed into the wagon. Blackie and Brownie barked and danced around. Josh let them climb into the wagon and they snuggled up to Rebecca.

Josh tied Spartan and Zeus to the back of the wagon then climbed onto the seat and picked up the ribbons. Mama and Cenora—and probably Stella—were meeting them at the ranch. Papa had said he was sorry he had to work at the barbershop, but of course people depended on him being available. She didn't know if Dallas and Finn would show up to lend a hand.

At the ranch, Grizzly greeted them. "Mercantile delivered a load of paint. Said it's from someone named Council Clayton 'cause he can't come out to help."

Josh hopped down and came around to help her. "Clayton is my father-in-law and he's the barber in town. Be a while before we can start on the outside, but that's real nice of him."

Grizzly chuckled and tugged on his beard. "Haven't

been to one of those in quite a while. Reckon I'll have to visit him 'fore too long if he's your kin. Today, I aim to help you folks unless you have something you'd rather me do."

"Strong backs welcome."

Mama and Stella arrived together only minutes before Dallas and Cenora.

Stella ran to her, her blue-green eyes sparkling. "Finn had to deliver a horse for Dallas but he'll be out later. This is so exciting. You'll have a lovely home close to ours and we'll both be close to Mama and Papa."

Nettie loaded her arms with supplies. "Someday this will be a wonderful home, but right now the inside is a pig pen. Honestly, that man Tyson deserves to be in jail for letting this lovely place get so dirty even if he weren't a criminal on other counts."

Mama, Stella, Rebecca, and Cenora followed with more cleaning equipment.

Inside, Nettie set down her things in the foyer. "Josh and I talked about this last night. I suggest we tackle one room at a time. The men can move furniture out of the room and then we can thoroughly clean. Each piece will need to be swept or polished before it goes back. There's a line in back where we can air the curtains."

"Sounds good." Stella picked up a delicate porcelain lamp with a decorated globe. "This looks like an antique. Shall I set it on the dining table?"

Before long, the parlor was empty and Josh cleaned the fireplace grate. The women raised the windows and were busily sweeping and dusting. After the room was clean, they lowered and polished windows. When the room was ready, they moved to the porch and started work on the furniture. Clouds of dust rose when they swept the upholstered pieces.

Once the room was restored, she and Josh stood admiring the parlor.

"Tempting to just go in and sit down, isn't it?" He had his arm around her waist.

Nettie leaned her head against his shoulder. "The room is even more beautiful than I'd imagined. I love this house."

Dallas bumped shoulders with his cousin. "Hey, you

two, stop daydreaming. There are a lot more rooms to clean. I need help moving this china cabinet out of the dining room."

Grizzly hurried through the door. "I can tackle that. Miss Jenny had me move it a time or two so she could clean. Comes apart into two pieces."

Puzzled, Nettie glanced at her husband. "I don't understand why Mr. Tyson didn't take more of his belongings."

Josh stood with his hands on his hips. "When foreclosure happens, the contents are part of the sale. Sometimes, they're auctioned off item by item or in lots, but this sale included everything because the creditors just wanted to get it over with as quickly as possible."

Nettie smiled at him. "Thank you for explaining. The sadness of the situation tinges my happiness at having this lovely home and beautiful things inside."

Grizzly said, "Now don't you fret, Miss Nettie. Bob knew the foreclosure was coming. He had plenty of time to sell off some things. Reckon the drink had affected his mind 'cause he refused to believe anyone could take his ranch away from him. Far as I know, he didn't try to salvage anything beforehand."

Nettie thought about the plans and care that had gone into building and furnishing this house. How sad that the place had been ravaged by time and lack of care. She wondered if Mrs. Tyson and the children yearned for their belongings they'd had to abandon.

She asked the huge man, "Do you have an address for Mrs. Tyson?"

He shook his head. "Miss Jenny said she was through with anything that reminded her of this place and her life here."

Mama exclaimed, "Oh, my, the china cabinet is filled with dishes that will have to be washed." She opened a drawer. "And silver to be polished."

Nettie peered inside the drawer. "Isn't this great? I didn't realize we had silver."

Stella said, "We should just set them aside and wash and polish them later. The sooner we get the actual house clean, the better."

Nettie turned with a stack of dinner plates in her hands. "I'd rather we wash them now. I want everything clean as we go."

All business, Mama surveyed the dinnerware. "This will take quite a while to wash but it should be done before it can go back into the cabinet."

Nettie started to speak, but Josh raised his hands. "Nettie's house, Nettie's rules."

Stella laughed. "I always forget that although I'm the oldest, I'm not her boss."

Mama, Stella, and Rebecca washed dishes and Cenora and Nettie cleaned the dining room. By noon, they'd only cleaned two rooms, the downstairs hall, and the foyer. Nettie's arms and back were tired from so much polishing.

Finn showed up while they were sitting on the front porch eating the lunch Kathryn and Emma had sent.

Grizzly joined them. "Sure nice to see the parlor windows shining. I'm real proud of what you folks are doing to this fine old place."

Nettie smiled at the man whose appearance yesterday had frightened her. "Sure nice to have your help."

Rebecca asked, "Are you named Grizzly because of your strength?"

He stroked his beard, his blue eyes twinkling. "Might be because of my good looks."

They finished downstairs, removed all the bedding and curtains from upstairs. In the master bedroom, Mama ruthlessly swept spiders out of corners.

Stella opened a dresser drawer and squealed. "Ugh, a nest of mice."

Grizzly apparently heard her. "I'll take care of those for you."

At five o'clock, Nettie surveyed the room. "This one is clean. I think we should stop for the day." She looked from one person to the other. "Thank you so much for your hard work."

Mama hugged Nettie's shoulders. "At least you could sleep here now. I guess you plan to go back to Kathryn and Austin's tonight."

"Yes, we do. And you have to go by and pick up

Lance."

Mama stepped back and peered at her. "You didn't see Austin send him home on a horse last night?"

Perplexed, Nettie shook her head. "No, I don't think I've seen him ride."

"He had to learn to do errands for Mr. Pratt at the livery. Mr. Pratt said he's a natural. Finn said the same thing."

"That's wonderful. Oh, Mama, I do hope he gets to go to medical school."

"I do too. Austin's paying him six bits a day to stay with Daniel. Can you imagine?"

Nettie eyes widened. "That's more than many grown men make. I'll bet Lance is pleased."

"He's over the moon, but his job won't be easy. He can barely lift Daniel from the chair to the bed and vice versa. He has to help him with his bodily functions, too, and with dressing."

"Lance will probably build up his muscles soon. Mama, I feel so sad for Daniel having to endure the indignity of not being able to care for himself. He's such a kind, gentle soul."

"The church women have started a prayer chain for him. We're all praying he'll walk again."

"That's good. There's never too much prayer, is there?"

"Dr. Sullivan's wife told me he's written away to some doctor famous for his treatment of paralysis. Dr. Sullivan explained Daniel's case and asked for an opinion."

"Oh, Kathryn will be so relieved to hear that."

Mama clasped her arm and shook her head. "I don't think you should tell her. If the doctor wants her to know, he will. Probably he doesn't want to get her hopes up in case the news is bad."

Nettie realized her error. "I can see that. While it would give her hope now, if the news is unfavorable later, she'd feel worse than ever."

"Exactly. Oh, well Stella's ready so I'll go. I'll be back tomorrow, dear."

Nettie hugged her mother and sister and Cenora. Then she and Rebecca climbed into the wagon and Josh drove them home. He left Spartan and Zeus in the barn under Grizzly's care.

Back at Kathryn and Austin's home, Nettie staggered to the mudroom. What she wouldn't give for a hot bath. When she entered the kitchen, she found Kathryn pouring hot water into a tub set behind a screen.

Her mother-in-law glanced up. "Emma and I figured you and Rebecca would be eager for a bath so we have one for you right here."

"You're a mind reader. But what about Rebecca?"

"She'll have her turn before bedtime. Knowing her, I wouldn't be surprised if she goes down to the river and dives in before then."

Nettie wasted no time before unbuttoning her brown dress. "I'm so grateful for all your help. The lunch was delicious. Honestly, I don't think I've ever been this dirty."

She stripped and sank into the steaming water. "Oh, this is heaven." A chair set near the tub and held a towel, sponge, and bar of soap. She sniffed the lavender fragrance and soaped her body.

From the other side of the screen, Kathryn said, "Emma and I have several boxes of food for you to take tomorrow. You'll have to send Josh to town for more supplies, but we've packed canned and dried fruits and vegetables as well as some root vegetables. Later, I'll come help you plant a herb and vegetable garden."

"You're so generous, but I accept the food. And we saw where a garden had been. The dill, fennel, and a couple of plants I couldn't identify were still growing but weeds had taken over."

"How much did you get cleaned?"

"All but four bedrooms, but that doesn't include the curtains. I hope there's no rain tonight because I left them airing on the line. That includes even the washable ones in hopes some of the dust will blow away before I launder them."

Josh came through the kitchen.

Kathryn said, "No men allowed, son."

"Hey, she's my wife." She heard the laughter in his voice. "I think you're showing favoritism over your own son to fix my wife a hot bath and leave me to the cold outside pump."

Smiling, she sank into the water. "You have my sympathy, husband."

"Yeah, yeah, wife. I can tell you're sincere." His boots thudded as he climbed the stairs.

Chapter Eighteen

The following morning, elation burst from Nettie. "We're moving into our own home. I'm so excited I can hardly stay still."

"I noticed, wife. You're dashing around until you're making me dizzy."

She sent him a knowing glance as she added the last item to a valise. "Don't tell me you're not excited too."

"Yeah, I am. This is a big step. I'm going from working with—for—Pa to being in charge. I mean, we still run the land as one ranch, but I'll be responsible for insuring that our share is profitable." He met her gaze. "What if I can't?"

"You'll do a good job. You've been ranching all your life and know all the ins and outs of making a ranch successful. Your mother is going to teach me how to do the things I'll need to be your wife and helpmate."

He picked up the two valises. "I sure hope you're right. Soon as I have a chance, I'll collect the rest of our things from the Tall Trees cabin."

She gazed around, making certain she hadn't forgotten anything. She'd stripped the bed and put on clean linens. Everything in Josh's former room was as tidy as when she'd first seen the room. With a light heart, she headed downstairs.

They bid everyone at the house goodbye and set out for their new home. Rebecca rode in the wagon, but her horse was tied behind so she'd have a way home later. Josh's spare horse was also tied to the back. He told her the wagon and two harnessed horses were also his.

Nettie gazed at her husband. "We need to think a different name than 'the new McClintock place' for our home."

Rebecca giggled. "How about Love Land."

Josh turned to glare at his sister but laughter laced his voice, "Very funny. How about No-Sisters-Allowed Land?"

The girl appeared to consider. "You could use

McClintock's North."

"Come on, Becky, you're more creative than that."

Nettie had thought about the name. "How about Joshua's?"

"Naw, that leaves out you."

They tossed names back and forth all the way to their home. The names became more ridiculous by the minute and Nettie laughed until tears filled her eyes. As they pulled into the homestead, the others had already arrived. Nettie and Rebecca hurried inside while Grizzly helped Josh carry in supplies.

Nettie put away food while her mother, sister, Rebecca, and Cenora cleaned. When she went upstairs, she could barely weave her way along the hall. At least two bedrooms of furniture lined the walls.

Mama waved at her. "That nice man helped Dallas and Finn set things out so we could get started. Stella and I arrived very early because we knew you wanted to finish today."

Cenora nodded. "I had the same idea. Ma and Da kept Houston overnight and saved me time. I thought Dallas and I might as well get started on your home."

Nettie saw the room had already been swept and walls brushed free of cobwebs. She picked up a bucket of vinegar water and set it near a window. "Kathryn sent a lot of food she and Emma had canned and dried."

Rebecca turned from polishing another window. "And me. I helped them."

She smiled at her sister-in-law. "I know you did, Becky. You help your mother a great deal." Popping her with a cleaning cloth, she said, "But you fail at ranch naming."

Rebecca giggled and dodged out of the way.

"Dallas and Finn brought proper shingles and are on the roof patching the leak. We're to call them if they're needed elsewhere."

Josh said, "Oh, man, that's a steep climb. I'd better see if they need help."

Mama stopped him. "Actually, we need you to set up the furniture in the second bedroom. We've finished cleaning there."

By two, inside the house was tidy and salvageable furniture set in place. Josh and Nettie stood on the wide veranda waving as their kin departed. Grizzly went to the barn to check on the horses so Josh and Nettie went inside.

"Well, Mrs. McClintock, our home is finally ours."

"I'm so excited. I know I said this before, but this is better than anything I ever dreamed."

"The best is yet to come." He took her hand. "Come with me."

Thinking he had something to show her, she climbed the stairs with him as he led her to their bedroom.

Gently, he cupped her face. "I've waited to make love to you here, in our own bed in our own room in our own home."

"How could any woman resist such a romantic declaration?" She met his lips.

He broke contact only to caress her while he rained kisses on her face and neck. "I want this to be perfect. We're in our own place where we have a future."

She trembled as she unbuttoned her dress.

Brushing away her hands, he whispered, "Let me."

He slipped her dress from her shoulders and it pooled at her feet. Her petticoat ties were next. She stepped from her dress and petticoat. He led her to the bed and turned back the cover. He lifted her onto the mattress and removed her shoes, then rolled down her stockings.

She threw off her chemise and drawers. In the broad daylight, her first thought was to cover herself with the sheet. Forcing herself to brazenly pose for his inspection, she leaned back on her elbows.

He'd removed most of his clothes but stopped to stare at her. His eyes watched her as if drinking her in. "You are even more gorgeous by daylight than lamplight. I'm a lucky man."

She smiled at the passion darkening his eyes. Her newfound power pleased and surprised her. How wonderful that her husband desired her.

"I'm a lucky woman, Josh McClintock." She removed the pins from her hair and lay back on the bed, making sure her tresses spread out on the pillow as he preferred.

Bare as a newborn, he stretched out beside her. The size of him no longer frightened her because she knew how well they fit. He leaned on an elbow.

Tentatively, she touched his chest. "I haven't touched you as much as I wished."

"We haven't made love very many times. When we have, we've both been tired and rushed. I'm sure you're exhausted now after all the cleaning. At least we have all the time in the world."

She laughed quietly. "I hope Grizzly doesn't interrupt us this time."

Caressing her arm, he leaned near her ear. "I told him we were taking the rest of the day off to enjoy our new home."

Gasping, she asked, "Do you think he suspects what we're doing?"

He chuckled. "He'd have to be dense if he doesn't and he appears to be a smart man. Don't worry about him. We have the right to enjoy each other's body."

She closed her eyes and felt heat from a blush stain her face. "How will I face him tomorrow knowing he guessed?"

"The way you faced him today. This is what married people do and no one thinks otherwise. Now, let's get back to where we were."

His mouth guided hers. Teasing, coaxing, he sucked her bottom lip, nipped at it. Her arms slid around his neck and she leaned to meet him. His tongue thrust between her teeth. Again and again, his tongue probed, tasted, teased.

No longer was his kiss soft or hesitant. The room swirled around her as she sank into his spell. In her wildest dreams she would never have imagined a kiss could ever be this potent.

Heat coiling in her core exploded and intensified. She couldn't get enough of him. Low moans came from her throat or his, she no longer cared. He broke the kiss to meet her gaze, his blue eyes dark with passion. He kissed his way to her breast, pulling her nipple into his mouth.

"I love when you do that." Raking her hands through his hair, she gasped in pleasure.

He moved to the other orb and held the first in his hand. She arched her back to offer up better access. While he continued to suckle her breast, his hand moved to the juncture of her thighs. He inserted a finger inside her folds while his thumb moved across her nub. She gasped with pleasure as her head thrashed on the pillow.

She craved more, more, more of this wonderful sensation. He released her breast and moved to reclaim her lips. He broke the kiss to move to her ear while he thrust himself against her hip.

She held him close to her, aching for his touch. The power of her desire astonished her. Was it the day's importance, being alone, or her growing love for her husband?

Whispering, he asked, "Can you feel what you do to me?"

She reached for his shaft, gripping gently with one hand. "Yes.

The fingers of her other hand probed the velvety tip. She massaged the bead of moisture that appeared. He closed his eyes and moaned. She smiled, pleased to return the pleasure he'd given her. Though her sister had hinted, no one had told her she had this control over her mate.

Grasping her hand, he said, "No more or this will be over before we've begun."

He kissed her and she opened her mouth to him. Rising above her, he pushed inside her. She thrust herself at him, eyes squeezed shut. Again and again he rocked into her, driving her to an ecstasy she could not have imagined.

Lost in the moment, she climbed higher and higher with each glorious movement. His breathing grew more labored as his thrusts increased in closeness. When she thought she would explode from sheer joy, her release erupted in waves. At the same time, she felt the burst of his seed explode within her.

Together they floated back to earth. She clung to him. He rolled off her but cuddled her to him. He kissed her hair and her face. She noted the trembling of his hands as they smoothed over her arms.

He had driven her wild with his touch, but she affected him too. She felt a woman desired. Perhaps he didn't return her love yet, but she believed they were on their way there.

He hugged her to his side. "That was the best ever."

Did he mean the best ever or the best with her? "And you didn't roll over and go to sleep. But you can now, husband. After all that excellent work, you must be tired."

He kissed her cheek. "Excellent, eh? Well, that's good to hear."

She snuggled against him. "Of course, I have a limited frame of reference, but I do judge that was your best effort."

Reaching down to tug at the cover, he pulled the sheet over them. "I believe a brief nap is in order before we go down for supper."

"With no curtains up, we certainly can't appear downstairs like this. Poor Grizzly might get the shock of his life."

She spooned to his side and closed her eyes. With a deep sigh, she smiled in contentment. Such a wonderful day must mean their troubles were over.

Chapter Nineteen

Standing on the wide veranda the following morning, Josh kissed Nettie goodbye. "Grizzly has the wagon hitched. We'll get your supplies and order the lumber and nails for repairs on the barn. Ought to be back by noon."

She handed him her list for the kitchen. "I've just enough soap left for the curtains and our laundry so I'll get started while you're gone. Likely take me all morning."

He laid his revolver on the kitchen table. "I'm leaving this in case anyone who shouldn't comes around. You know how to aim. I'll buy you your own revolver but this will have to do today."

"I'm sure I'll be fine. After all, the only ne'er do well is in jail."

He held her shoulders to meet her gaze. "Tyson's not the only dangerous man in Texas. Keep the revolver with you just to humor me. Okay?"

Although she nodded, he knew she wasn't fond of the idea. "I'll keep it in my pocket, but it's awfully heavy."

"I'll find you a smaller gun." He kissed her again. "We won't be gone long."

She gazed up at him, her blue eyes sparkling with mischief. "Then you'd better get started, husband."

"Why do I think you forget who's head of this household, wife?"

She sent him a flirty smile. "Dear husband, I haven't forgotten."

He gave her a shake of his head. "That's what I'm afraid of, wife."

Hopping off the veranda, he strode to the wagon and climbed onto the seat. With a wave, he and Grizzly were off toward town.

They stopped at the lumberyard first where he ordered a load of lumber, nails, and assorted other hardware needed for the barn and outbuildings. Neptune and Poseidon were strong horses, but he didn't want them pulling lumber and his wagon wasn't strong enough for all he needed anyway.

"Anything we need to get for your place, Grizzly?"

The big man tugged at his beard. "Reckon I can use some of the shingles your kin had left from yesterday?"

"Of course. Anything else?" Josh had a feeling he needed to visit the interior of Grizzly's house to assess the condition.

"Reckon there'll be left over from this lumber? I got some loose boards."

Josh adjusted the order and included extra.

"Miss Nettie going to repaper the rooms?"

Josh figured that meant Grizzly's house needed new wallpaper. "Yes, but that'll happen later. For now, we're just repairing damage."

They stopped by the livery to inquire of Fred Brewster if anyone was looking for ranch work.

"Yep, they's a couple of guys staying at the hotel. All I know about them is the names Stu and Lucky. Horses look good, well cared for. Nothing too fancy about the saddles but in good shape. Oh, speak of the devil, here they come now."

Josh introduced himself and Grizzly. The men looked hungry, but not disreputable.

"You guys on the move or looking to settle down?"

The one named Stu rubbed his chin. He was clean-shaven and lean and looked to be about twenty. "I have a girl here. She was visiting the ranch where I worked before, but had to come home. I followed. If I find a decent job, we're getting hitched."

"You plan on living on the ranch or getting your own place?"

"I won't lie to you, mister. I want a house where Peggy and I can live. Not sure I could run my own place without going bust like my pa did. I can work hard, though, and I ride for the brand."

Josh addressed the other man. "What about you, Lucky? What's your story?"

Lucky looked to be mid-twenties and was several

inches shorter than Josh. His stocky build looked strong. His brown hair was a little long, but appeared clean enough.

"Not much to tell. Met Stu on the trail. Man I worked for since I was fourteen sold out and the new owner had his own hands. New man said I was a good worker, he just didn't need me. Gave me a letter saying as much. I ride for the brand, too, mister."

"You mind waiting here while I confer with my foreman?" He moved about twenty feet away and asked Grizzly, "Well, what do you think?"

"Seem nice enough, but you can't never go by what folks say. Okay with me if you want to give them two a try. We can see how they work."

Josh went back to the two. "Why don't you settle up with the hotel and get your gear. I'll be at the mercantile loading up on supplies. You meet me there soon as you can."

Both men broke into wide grins and claimed their horses.

Grizzly drove the wagon and he rode on the seat. The two new cowboys passed them heading for the hotel.

Grizzly flicked the reins. "Get the feeling they're relieved to have a job."

"Be scary being without one, especially if you wanted to get married. I was nervous just not having a house where I could take my wife."

"You sure got one now. Rate you're going, 'fore long it'll be a showplace."

"That's my plan." Josh's thoughts turned to his life with Nettie.

He should have told her he'd fallen in love with her. Why couldn't he say the words? He'd sure as hell resented having to marry her, but now he realized she'd saved him. Now he knew Pa wouldn't have given him the ranch if he hadn't changed his ways.

If Nettie were gone, he'd miss her. She was bad-tempered and bossy, but she was also funny and smart. Life with her would never be boring.

He gave his wife's list to Otto Roan, the mercantile owner. Killing time while Otto filled the list, he browsed through the store. He spied fabric and thought of his wife. He knew she only had three or four dresses. What he knew about dresses was how fast it took to get a woman out of one.

Sara Roan asked, "Need some help?"

He jumped then touched a bolt of lilac. "Um, how much of that would it take to make a woman's dress?"

She smiled and warmth radiated from her brown eyes. "You want me to measure it off for you? I could also measure off the trim that matches."

"Yes, ma'am. That and what goes with it to make a nice dress." What was wrong with him? He didn't even know if Nettie liked lavender. He knew she sewed, because he'd seen her mend things.

Sara got busy and soon had a package tied up in brown paper. "Anything else?"

"You have any shirts that fit Grizzly?"

She nodded. "We keep a couple in his size. Yours, too."

"I'll take the two in his size. What else you have that fits him?"

"One pair of pants and three pairs of socks and a couple pairs of drawers."

He made a sweeping motion. "Put 'em in. He stuck with the ranch when everyone else deserted. I figure he deserves a bonus."

Now he knew he'd gone round the bend. Since when did he start shopping for others? His idea of generosity had been buying a round of drinks. Nettie had changed him. He hoped his foreman didn't get mad at him for interfering in his business.

When he went back outside, he found the two new hires waiting for him. "You fellas need anything before we start for the ranch?"

Both looked down and answered no. Josh figured that meant they were broke. Grizzly checked the wagon load to be sure everything would ride well.

He slapped a palm to his forehead. "Dang, we haven't cleaned the bunkhouse yet. Fellas, don't be upset at the state of things. The bunkhouse has been deserted—"

Grizzly raised his hand. "I cleaned it yesterday

afternoon. Reckon it ain't too fancy, but it's clean."

"Thanks, Grizzly. That makes me even happier I bought you a couple of shirts for being so loyal while the place was empty."

The big man's eyes grew wide. "You got me something?"

He ran his fingers over the packages. "Sure did. This package right here must be yours."

"Well, I'll swan. Ain't nobody never give me a present."

"Then it's time someone did."

Lester Higgins ran into the street yelling, "Jail break. The men in jail have broken out. Send for the doc, Sheriff Yates is wounded."

Josh froze. Jail break meant Tyson was loose. Josh ran to intercept Lester. "Is Tyson gone?"

Without stopping, Lester called, "And his buddies. Must have had help."

Grizzly climbed onto the wagon. "We got to get home."

He vaulted onto the wagon. "Damn right." To his new cowboys, he said, "I hope you have firepower with you."

Kurt Tomlinson rode toward him. "Just heard, I'm going with you. Dorcas has gone to warn your folks."

Council ran from the barbershop and caught onto the side of the wagon. He couldn't climb on with it moving but sort of rolled over the side to the bed. "Heard Lester yelling. Don't have a gun, but I'm going with you."

By now the wagon was moving at top speed. Poseidon and Neptune were strong horses and sped through town and toward the ranch.

Josh wished he'd ridden Spartan into town. By now he'd be home and have his rifle with him. His rifle—if Tyson went through the barn, he'd find the rifle in the saddle scabbard. Josh had stashed another inside the house, but he'd forgotten to tell Nettie where it was.

They had to get there. As they passed farmhouses, Josh yelled at the residents. A few men joined with them, others ran inside to fortify their own homes. By the time they turned into the drive to his home, there were ten in their party. He knew

Lester would be following with whoever he could raise as a posse.

He pictured all the harm that could befall Nettie and almost lost his mind.

Council placed a hand on his shoulder. "Don't think about anything but getting there, son. I know you taught Nettie to shoot. Does she have a gun with her?"

"Yes, but what good will a revolver be against several men? Especially when she doesn't even know Tyson is free?"

"She's not defenseless and she's a smart woman. We have to take comfort from that."

Chapter Twenty

Nettie sorted her laundry while waiting for water in the large black pot to boil beside the one she'd filled with cold water for rinsing. She had always hated washing clothes, second only to ironing. Both chores were hot, backbreaking work. She shaved soap into the pot and stirred with a long stick.

Starting with her unmentionables, she finished them and set them in the basket. Next she did her husband's and set them aside to hang with hers. She sighed, the curtains were next. While they soaked, she hung her things on the line. Smiling, she wondered if the men would be embarrassed by her chemises and drawers.

The curtains were easy to get clean but difficult to handle. Many were lace and she was careful not to tear the delicate weave. She was happy when that part of her chore was on the line drying. Standing back, she took pride in the bright whites.

Sheets were next. Many were so dirty she feared they'd disintegrate from rot when they hit the water. She stirred and lifted and wrung until her hands were red and burning. Her brow was dripping with perspiration and it ran down her back and pooled under her arms. The ground around the huge black kettles had become muddy and surrounded by puddles. She should have planned two days for this many things.

The curtains dried by the time she had the sheets washed. Good thing because there was no more space. She carefully folded the lace panels and hung the sheets. Sure enough several had tears where the fabric had simply given way. Sad when dirt held cloth together. Still, some might be mended and others could be used for bandages or cleaning cloths.

Carrying the dried lace and her chemises and drawers, she went inside to cool off. After putting away her unmentionables, she sat at the kitchen table and sipped cold water. She'd just washed her face and hands in cool water when she heard the sound of hoof beats. She listened, not wagon wheels, but horses.

Quickly, she picked up the revolver and went to the back door. Her heart jumped to her throat. Four men rode into the yard. She suspected she knew who they were.

Dear Lord in Heaven, help me. What chance do I have?

Knees so wobbly they would hardly support her, she closed and locked the door, then ran to do the same with the front and side doors. Not that she could keep the men out, but she could slow them down. At least, she hoped she could. With all the glass, there was no way to keep them from entering.

When she returned to the kitchen, one of the men was at the back door. He turned the knob and shook it.

She picked up her meat cleaver. He broke the back door's window and reached through. She slammed down the sharp cleaver with all her force.

A scream shrieked and blood dripped from the glass and cleaver. He cradled his dripping hand and screamed obscenities. She hadn't severed his limb but had done enough damage he wouldn't be firing a gun with that hand anytime soon even if the blood loss didn't kill him.

She laid the cleaver in the sink and showed herself with the gun pointed at the door. "This isn't your place any longer and you should never have broken the glass. Get out while you can."

"Who the hell are you?" Called a short, tubby man whose hand was bandaged.

"The owner of this house. Now leave."

A taller man asked, "Where's Grizzly?"

"None of your business, is it? This is my ranch now and you have no right to be here. Leave or I shoot."

She advanced on the door hoping the men didn't hear her heart pounding. Aiming through the broken glass, she fired at the tall man's arm. She missed and hit his knee.

"Yeow! The bitch hit me on my good leg." He sat on the porch and cradled his knee. Blood stained his pants where the bullet had stuck.

"Next one will be higher. Anyone want to see?"

A mustached man called, "Listen, lady, this here's our place and we want in. We know you're alone so you might as well give up now or we'll have to kill you."

She answered by firing at his stomach but hit his arm. He rewarded her by cussing her and all her family. Where had the tubby man gone? She whirled to find him pointing a gun at her.

Without thinking, she pulled the trigger. Surprise spread across his face and his gun went off, the bullet striking the floor as he fell.

Dear Merciful God, forgive me. Have I killed a man?

She raced to kick his weapon away from his reach. She picked up the gun and watched the back door. Mustache man's face appeared.

She kept her revolver aimed at him. "You'd better go for the doctor. Your friend is hit bad."

"Who the hell are you?"

"Nettie Sue McClintock. My husband Josh and I own this spread. Now leave while you're able."

She heard the man with the injured hand. "It's the wife of that McClintock's whelp. Get her boys. She can't hold out against four of us."

She went to the door. "I can hold out longer than you can. You'd better leave while you're able to ride."

She heard a noise behind her and turned.

The tubby man rose on one elbow. "Help me, Bob. You got to get me a doc."

She stepped back and to the side so she could watch the door and the tubby man. "You heard your friend. He's bleeding all over my clean floor. That's right, my *clean* floor. How could you live in such filth? You must be part pigs."

"This is my ranch." A man screamed, "This is my ranch and nobody has a right to say otherwise. I built this house and the barns."

"You should have thought of that before you gambled and drank up all your resources. Now take your medicine like a man and leave. You no longer own this ranch and have no right to be here."

"I'll show you. I'll burn this place down before I let a McClintock live here."

She recalled the wash pot fire she'd left burning. Opening the door, she shot at the man hobbling toward the fire. She missed but he dove for cover. The tall man lunged at her, but she fired. He was so close she couldn't miss and hit his arm.

The mustached man reached for her.

She pointed her gun at him. "You sure you want to do that?"

"You don't have any bullets left."

"Yes, I do. Want to see?" One. She had only one bullet left.

"You're bluffing." He reached through the glass to open the door.

She fired at him. The bullet zinged by, grazing his ear. He smiled as if she were caught in a snare, not even bothering to brush away the blood dripping from the injury. He'd opened the door.

She showed him the gun she'd picked up from the floor.

He froze, a perplexed expression on his face.

She faced him. "Get out or you won't be able to. Are you so stupid you can't learn a lesson?"

The tubby man cried, "Rex, go for the doc. Man, I'm hurtin' somethin' awful."

The sound of wagon wheels accompanied riders. She clutched the gun with both hands as the commotion drew closer. The men on her porch were surrounded.

Josh rushed into the kitchen, gun drawn. Her father followed behind her husband.

Josh looked the way he had the day Daniel was injured. He reached for her. "Thank God, Nettie. I was afraid we wouldn't get here in time."

She let the gun dangle from one hand while she rushed into Josh's arms. "I was afraid of the same thing."

As if he just saw over her shoulder, he pulled her to his side. "What the hell happened here?"

"Y-You told me to shoot if I needed to. And I did." Her

legs would no longer support her and she sank onto a chair.

"Are you all right?" He knelt and touched her face then her shoulders as he looked her up and down from head to toe.

She braced her hands on his arms. "I'm fine, or as all right as a person can be who's just shot three men and about chopped off another's hand."

Her father kneeled beside her. "Nettie, we were so worried."

She forced a tremulous smile for him. "I'm all right now, Papa."

The tubby man cried, "Someone please get me a doctor."

Josh stood and glared. "My compassion doesn't extend to a man who'd try to hurt a woman. You'll have to wait until the posse gets here."

Nettie rose on wobbling legs. "He's losing a lot of blood, Josh. We should help him so he doesn't die in our kitchen. That'd be a sad start for our new home."

"If you insist, but I'd let the bastard suffer. He certainly intended to harm you."

She hadn't the energy to go to the clothesline for worn sheets and gathered a couple of clean tea towels and a pan of water. "I know, but that's on him. What I do about his injury is on me. I don't want to have killed a man."

"Let me help you in case he tries anything."

The tubby man lay on his side. "I'm hurtin' bad and can barely breathe. I sure ain't going to hurt anyone who tries to help me."

When Josh and Papa turned the man over, he moaned and clutched his side.

Nettie set down the pan of water and cloths. "Gut shot?"

Papa shook his head. "More like a kidney or liver. He'll live long enough to go to prison."

She set to work cleaning the wound. The bullet had lodged in his side about where she thought the liver was. If Kathryn were here she would be able to help the man.

Grizzly came into the kitchen and chuckled. "Miss Nettie, you sure surprised those men. Guess they'll be glad to get back to jail where they're safe."

He stood over the tubby man. "You know better than to try hurtin' a woman like this, Fred. What got into your head?"

The tubby man's head rolled to the side. "Bob had me. Owe him money and can't pay. He said I had to help him get back his ranch. Knew we couldn't. Said he'd shoot me if I didn't pay up or pitch in with him."

The foreman shook his head. "You'd of been better off just shootin' Bob."

"Rex woulda killed me. You know his temper and he's better with a gun than I am."

While they talked, Nettie had been sponging off blood and examining the wound. "You need the lead dug out. I've never done anything like that, but I've seen my mother-in-law perform the procedure."

Josh touched her hand. "I have too. I'll help you if you're determined to save this man."

"Please, lady. I'm sorry for scaring you. I wouldn't have shot you, honest."

Josh glared at the man. "Just shut up if you know what's good for you. Don't keep playing the innocent victim."

Papa looked fierce and kicked the man's hip. "You knew the others would have killed her after attacking her first."

The injured man cried, "I'm sorry, I'm sorry. Please help me and I'll never do nothing like this again."

Josh said, "You've got that right. From now on you'll be in jail and then prison if you're lucky. If I had my way, you'd all hang."

Papa said, "I never thought I could say this, but I could strangle you with my bare hands right here. You'd better be thankful my daughter has a compassionate nature."

Trying to ignore the talk going on around her, Nettie looked up at Grizzly. "You have any alcohol in your house? I need something to clean the wound."

"I'll get my bottle." He left.

Josh stood. "I'll put water on to boil. Nettie, you have any idea what you're going to use to dig out the lead?"

She'd been considering what they had in the house. She'd need a knife to enlarge the wound, but how could she grip the metal to extract it from the opening? Kathryn had used medical instruments.

She rose and looked at her husband, who was filling the kettle with water. "I'll use two knives." After pulling open a cupboard drawer, she rummaged through the utensils. "Ah, here we are, two small paring knives may work."

Nettie lit a candle and ran the blades back and forth through the flame. "Josh, I'll need a bit of the flour you bought today to staunch the blood and your mother sent some salve."

"I'll fetch flour for you. We probably jarred the sack's stitching loose. When we heard Tyson had escaped, we took off for here. Surprised the wagon didn't lose a wheel or break apart." He left the house but soon returned with an armload of supplies.

Grizzly also returned carrying a bottle of whiskey that looked about two-thirds full.

Nettie hoped her hands would be steady. Her insides quivered and knotted. What if her hands slipped and she made the injury worse? She took a deep, calming breath.

Josh knelt on the patient's other side. How she appreciated his support. Taking in and exhaling another long breath, she began.

She tore off a strip of toweling and folded it. "Bite on this. This is going to hurt, but I'll be as fast and gentle as I can."

"Just get on with it, ma'am." Tubby man, apparently really Fred, closed his eyes and bit down on the cloth.

Working quickly as she could, Nettie probed and found the small metal deposit. Her stomach roiled at the odor and sight. She wanted to retch, but forced herself to keep going.

Josh spoke low, "You're doing fine, Nettie."

He must have seen the panic on her face. She glanced up at him. "Found it, now all I have to do is get the thing out without causing more damage."

He nodded, a slight smile encouraging her. "Your patient appears to have passed out. Just as well."

She heard a commotion outside, but couldn't stop to see what had happened.

As if he read her mind, Josh said, "Posse arrived. Guess

they'll have to use the wagon to take this man to town."

She used two knives to lift the metal shard from the opening. Her hands shook and she lost grip on the bullet."

"You're doing fine. Just stay calm." Josh's voice calmed and reassured her.

This time she got the lead out of the man and dropped the metal remains on the floor. "Grizzly, I need that whiskey now."

He uncorked the bottle and handed it to her. "Wouldn't hurt you to take a swallow."

After managing a smile for him, she poured the alcohol on the wound.

Tubby man moaned and bucked even though he'd passed out. When she applied the flour and salve, he quieted down.

"I hate that I'm ruining our new tea towels, but there's no helping it." She made a compress of one towel and used strips of others to bind the pad in place.

Not until she leaned back did she notice the deputy standing nearby. He tipped his hat. "Right nice job, ma'am. We'll cart him off to jail now."

"He needs stitches but I don't have my sewing supplies with me."

Josh came around and helped her rise.

She looked at the man on the floor. "Doctor Sullivan will need to check him. I had no idea what I was doing."

Lester Higgins hooked his thumbs on his suspenders. "You sure saved us some work by corralling those men. That was quite some shooting you did."

Josh held her against him as she shuddered and tears poured from her eyes.

Clinging to her husband, she shook her head. "I did a terrible job, but I wanted to defend our home. We worked so hard to get it all nice. Mr. Tyson broke the window that was sparkling clean. I hit his hand with a meat cleaver when he reached through to unlock the door."

The deputy said, "He'll recover. Won't be using a gun with that hand ever again."

"Josh tried to teach me to shoot, but aiming at a person

is lots different from a tree branch. I meant to shoot one man's arm and hit his knee, then I did shoot his arm when he went to set fire to the house."

She wiped her tears with her arm. "I aimed at that scary man's belt buckle and hit his arm and then his ear. When this man surprised me, I jumped and fired without even intending to. I-I could have killed him." She turned her face into her husband's chest.

"Miz McClintock, don't you feel a bit bad. You saved your house and probably your life. For sure you'd have been hurt bad. Tyson is more than half crazy. A smart man would have headed as far away from here as he could. If those men had been inside, we'd have had to shoot the place up to get 'em out."

To Josh, the deputy lowered his voice and said, "That fool with the mustache is Rex Walker. He's wanted all over the state for a number of serious crimes. Your wife'll have a reward coming."

Two men from the posse lifted the unconscious tubby man and took him out as Josh's family entered.

Kathryn rushed to hug Nettie. "Rebecca and I were out delivering a baby and didn't get the news until Austin found me. We had no idea you were here fighting those men off on your own."

Austin appeared aghast at the blood on the floor and door. "I knew Tyson would take out his hatred of me on Kathryn and Rebecca if he found them. Dear Lord, Nettie, I had no idea you were here alone. You could have been killed."

Josh kept his arm around her. "Others joined us as we headed this way, Pa. In the meantime, Nettie held them off."

"I used all my bullets. If I hadn't taken the gun of the man in here, that awful mustached-man would have come in." She shivered. "The leer in his evil eyes scared me half out of my skin."

Josh caressed her arm. "You're safe now. Sorry you had to face them alone. I should have left the dogs here."

She shook her head. "Those men would have shot them."

He kissed her temple. "Can't tell you how proud I am

of you."

Kathryn appeared exhausted. Dark circles ringed her eyes. "Son, I know of a woman who would be willing to help Nettie here in the house. She'd live in like Emma."

Josh looked at Nettie. "I don't know, Mama. I just ordered a load of lumber and stocked up on supplies, plus hired two men. If I keep spending and we don't have a good year, I'm liable to be in trouble."

He raked a hand through his hair. "On the other hand, I sure don't want Nettie here by herself ever again."

After today, Nettie didn't want to be alone either, but she wasn't sure she wanted anyone living with her and Josh so early in their marriage.

She forced a smile and hoped she sounded more confident than she felt. "Don't worry, Josh. I don't mind being here on my own since that Tyson and his friends will be in jail."

Kathryn looked fierce. "Then I'll hire the woman as my housewarming gift. You also need a man who stays on the homestead and takes care of things around the house and barns while you and the others are working on the range."

Austin took his cue. "I'll hire that man for you. Better, you and Grizzly hire him and I'll pay his first year's salary."

Two men entered. A tall, thin one with blond hair tipped his hat to her then looked at Josh. "Boss, we figured Miz McClintock shouldn't have to clean up all that blood. Reckon she'd let us while you take her into the parlor?"

"Stu, thank you. Everyone, this is Stu and the fella with him is Lucky. They're the men I hired this morning. Sounds like I made a good choice."

Kathryn took Rebecca's hand. "Let's all go into the parlor before these nice men change their minds."

Chapter Twenty One

The next morning, Nettie avoided looking at the floor and back door while she prepared and served breakfast. Her dreams had been filled with horrible men chasing her. She was grateful Stu and Lucky had scrubbed for her.

Even though no trace of blood remained and a piece of burlap was tacked over the broken glass, yesterday's horror was too fresh in her mind. She'd had to force herself into the kitchen to cook breakfast for Josh and the men.

Josh carried his plate to the sink. "Good biscuits, wife."

The other three men stood and followed suit. Each had complimented her on the meal while they ate. The two new hires ate as if they hadn't had enough food for a quite a while.

Her husband grasped her shoulders. "We'll be working around the place today within easy hearing if you need me. Gonna start with the barn. Pa's sending over some hay later."

The longer she worked in the kitchen the less frightening the room became. She ironed and put the clean sheets on the beds. For a hearty lunch, she served ham and several of the canned vegetables Kathryn had given her as well as cornbread. She cleaned up the kitchen then ironed and hung the lace panels.

After tipping out the dirty wash water, she refilled the tub and built the fire. Their clothes were sorted in the mudroom. She washed her shirts, petticoats, and skirts.

She came in from hanging them on the line to get a cool glass of water and sit for five minutes.

Josh came up behind her and slid his hands around her waist. He nuzzled her neck.

She turned into his arms and they exchanged a searing kiss.

Tilting her head, she gazed at him. "Is something wrong? You have the strangest expression on your face."

He didn't meet her eyes. "Nothing's wrong. I just have

to ride into town on an errand."

"You want company? I could tidy up and go with you?"

"Not this time. Rush trip." He kissed her forehead. "I'll be back before dark."

"All right, I'll keep going on the house. Tomorrow I'm going to start on that beautiful lavender fabric you brought me. That was a lovely surprise."

He gripped her arms gently and met her gaze. "You know, honey, you don't have to work so hard. You could read or take a nap."

She touched his jaw then stepped back to stare at his face. "Josh, are you sure everything's all right?"

He clapped his hat on his head. "Positive."

Puzzled by his unusual behavior, she decided to finish her laundry. She'd brought in the clothes from yesterday, but hadn't washed any more. After the day's horrors, she had hardly been able to stand, much less work. Kathryn had prepared yesterday's lunch and cooked enough for supper too.

With Josh gone, she might as well keep busy. Humming a tune, she went through Josh's pockets before she took them to the yard. In one she found a crumpled pink piece of paper.

For a few minutes she stared at the wadded ball. She remembered seeing Dallas slip Josh something pink at the Tomlinson home and had caught the name "Isobel". Thinking back, she remembered seeing Isobel pat his shirt pocket at the Independence Day celebration. That nervy woman had probably slipped a note to him with her watching. Smoothing out the paper, she gasped.

I miss you, Josh, honey, and the fun we have together. When will I see you again—alone?

I.

Stunned, she rose and stuffed the note into her pocket. How many of these had Isobel sent? That must be why he went into town. She'd bet he'd be visiting that woman. Had he actually been working on the range all those times he was gone or had he made a trip to see her?

After the sweet lovemaking they'd shared in this home, how could he go see Isobel? Just when she thought they were making progress, she learned he'd played her for a fool. And she'd almost told him she loved him last night. Wouldn't he have laughed at that?

She took off her apron and changed into her split skirt. Shoving the note into her purse, she stomped to the barn. As she passed them, she nodded at the three men working. Without explanation, she threw Zeus' blanket on him.

Grizzly said, "Let me do that for you, ma'am." He proceeded to add the halter she'd forgotten and quickly saddled her horse.

"Thank you. I'm going to visit my mother. Would you put out the fire under the wash water, Grizzly? I forgot until now. If I'm not back by the time you're hungry, there's leftovers in the pantry."

The foreman held her horse while she mounted. "Sure thing, Miss Nettie. You have a nice visit."

So much for "forsaking all others." Josh hadn't meant his marriage vows at all. Why did he bother to lie? Why couldn't he have been honest and told her theirs was a marriage in name only?

By the time she got to her parents' home, her face was wet with tears. She spotted Josh's horse tied in front of Isobel's house. She looped Zeus's reins around her parents' fence and ran inside.

Her mother heard her enter and came to meet her. "Why, what's wrong, Nettie? Has something happened to Josh?"

She opened her purse and pulled out the hideous pink note. "Not yet, but it's about to."

Her mother read the note and handed it back to her. "But this doesn't prove he acted on the note. He even crumpled it…unless that's your work."

"That little message was wadded up in his pocket." She pointed next door. "But his horse is tied up in front of her house, so that proves he followed up, doesn't it?"

"Nettie, I've seen the way he looks at you. He loves you. I know he used to associate with her, but this doesn't sound like him now. You have to give Josh a chance to explain."

"Oh, I'll give him a chance to account for his actions. I'm going over there right now and tell them both what I think about their deception."

"Nettie, wait…" Her mother's voice faded.

Nettie marched out the front door and to the next house. Without knocking, she stormed into Isobel Hamilton's parlor. Josh stood near the unlit fireplace and Isobel sat on the sofa.

He frowned. "Nettie? Honey, what are you doing here?"

"I might ask you the same question, Joshua McClintock, but I know what you're doing." She threw the crumpled pink note at him. Then she turned and ran back to her parents' house.

"Nettie, wait!" Boot steps pounded after her.

In her split skirt, she outran him and slammed the door behind her and turned the lock.

He banged. "Nettie, I can explain. You didn't see what you think you did. Let me in."

"Go away. You can take Zeus with you because I won't be needing him now that I'll be living here at my parents' home."

She heard him conversing with someone. Glancing at the mantel clock, she thought Papa must be home for the day. Before her father could enter, she ran up the stairs to her old room and closed the door.

Soon Papa knocked. "Open this door and come downstairs."

"Please go away. Mama will tell you what happened. I don't want to talk to anyone right now."

"Nettie Sue Clayton McClintock, open this door this minute." Papa only used her full name when he was angry, and he sure sounded that way now.

Ha, she was the one who had reason to be angry. He should have listened and not insisted she and Josh marry. None of this would have happened then.

Sighing, she rose and opened the door.

Her father stood in the hall with his arms crossed. "What are you doing up here?"

"I'm moving home with you and Mama."

Slowly, he shook his head. "No, you're not. You're married and you belong with your husband. You *will* talk to him and work out your problems."

Shocked, she stared at him. "Papa? I'm your daughter. How can you turn me away?"

Mama hovered behind Papa. She leaned forward and whispered something to him.

He exhaled. "You can spend tonight since it would be dark before you arrived home. One night, do you understand?" He shook his forefinger at her. "First thing in the morning, you'll go to the home you share with your husband and reach a solution."

She stood with hands fisted. "He promised to forsake all others and I caught him at Isobel Hamilton's."

"And you promised "to honor until death do you part". Or have you forgotten that?"

"He lied to me."

Papa shook his head. "You're talking to the wrong person. This is between you and your husband. You can discuss the problem with him tomorrow when you go to your home."

How could her own sweet father turn her away? She drew herself up with all the dignity she could muster. "Good night, Mama and Papa."

As soon as she closed the door, she broke out into tears and collapsed onto her bed. The scent of roses reached her, reminding her of the night when Josh had climbed through her window. That only depressed her more. How could her life have become so messed up in such a short time?

Miserable, she wondered where she could go. Perhaps Stella and Finn would let her stay with them until she could find a teaching position elsewhere. The thought of leaving McClintock Falls pierced her heart like a knife.

Nettie loved living in this community, loved being near all her family. She loved her in-laws, loved her new home. More, she loved her husband who'd been unfaithful.

What was she to do?

After trying to read but only moping for an hour, she took off her skirt and shirt, stockings and half-boots. She'd have to sleep in her chemise until she could collect her clothes from the Tall Trees cottage and the ranch.

Humiliation and pain filled her thoughts. She'd lose Kathryn and Austin. She hoped Lance wouldn't lose his job working for Daniel. Probably Cenora and Dallas would shun her now, too. And the Tomlinsons and Gibsons she'd just found as friends. What would the people at church think?

And Josh? She had fallen so in love with her husband. His betrayal hurt more than anything she'd ever experienced. How could she stop loving him after she'd discovered how good a man he was. Except for his weakness for Isobel.

Nettie couldn't compete with a coquette like that woman. Isobel knew how to entice men to do as she wished. Obviously, Nettie didn't. Besides, she didn't want to trick Josh into wanting her. She needed him to desire her but for doing so to be his idea.

Lying in bed, she listened to the night sounds. A rattling reached her and she stilled. Could it be?

A figure climbed through the window and approached her bed.

She sat up. "You go right back out that window or I'll call my father."

"What will he do? He doesn't own a gun. He might make me marry you. Oh, wait, I believe we're already married." Josh sat on the bed and pulled off his boots and socks.

She tried kicking him off the bed. He didn't appear affected. Instead, he rose and took off his shirt and stepped out of his pants.

She crossed her arms. Even though it was too dark for him to see her expression, she glared at him. "I'm serious, Josh McClintock. You leave this room immediately."

"Can't. My wife's here." He climbed between the sheets and put his arms around her.

"You lied to me." She tried to push his arms away from her, but he held fast. She stiffened like a board with her hands fisted at her side.

He responded by merely caressing her and kissing her shoulder. "Didn't. If you'd have let Isobel or me explain, you'd have learned that I only went there to tell her to quit sending me notes."

"You didn't. I've seen the way she looks at you and the way you look back."

He paused. "How do we look?"

"She looks at you as if you were a delicious dessert and she was starving. You look at her as if you were a child receiving a special toy at Christmas."

"Wow, I had no idea you'd studied others." He resumed kissing he neck and shoulder.

"Make fun if you wish, but I'm staying right here at my parents' home or else with my sister. You might as well leave."

"Can't. This is where my wife is and I can't live without her. If you stay here, then I'll just have to climb in your window every night until you decide to come home."

"Why? I know you intended to visit Isobel the night you came here by mistake. You might as well go next door and spend the night there with the woman you really want."

"Did you not listen? I told you I went to tell her to quit sending me notes. She apologized. She knew why we got married and thought I wouldn't let a wedding change my way of life. When I told her I love you, she said I would never hear from her again. Even offered to come explain to you but I told her that wouldn't be necessary."

She turned to face him. "You told her what?"

"That her coming here wouldn't be necessary.

She pounded on his shoulder. "No, before that, before she said you'd never hear from her again."

"You heard me, wife. I love you."

She threw her arms around his neck. "Oh, Josh, I love you too. I thought you wished all this time you could be with Isobel. That you only viewed me as a…an unwanted complication."

"By now you should know I don't think of you in that way. I've admired you since I met you, but I didn't want to fall in love. I couldn't help myself."

He kissed her but broke away to say, "My reluctant bride, you're everything I could ever want in a woman. I want to spend my life with you, want you to be the mother of my children."

"That's what I want too. Shall we go home?"

He kissed her neck then moved to her shoulder. "Tomorrow, wife. I'm too busy right now."

Dear Reader,

If you'd like to know about my new releases, contests, giveaways, and other events, please **sign up for my newsletter here**.

Thank you for reading my book. If you enjoyed this story, please leave a review wherever you purchased the book. You'll be helping me and I'll appreciate your effort. So will prospective readers.

McCLINTOCK'S RELUCTANT BRIDE

Read Caroline's Amazon bestselling western historical titles:

The Most Unsuitable Wife, Kincaids book one

The Most Unsuitable Husband, Kincaids book two

The Most Unsuitable Courtship, Kincaids book three

Gabe Kincaid, Kincaids book four

Brazos Bride, Men of Stone Mountain book one
Buy the Audiobook here

High Stakes Bride, Men of Stone Mountain book two
Buy the Audiobook here

Bluebonnet Bride, Men of Stone Mountain book three

Tabitha's Journey, a Stone Mountain mail-order bride novella

The Texan's Irish Bride, McClintocks book one

O'Neill's Texas Bride; McClintocks book two

Save Your Heart For Me, a western adventure novella

Happy Is The Bride, a sweet humorous wedding novella

Long Way Home, a sweet Civil War adventure novella

Caroline's Time Travel

Out Of The Blue, 1845 Irish lass comes forward to today

Caroline's Contemporary Titles

Be My Guest, mildly sensual

Snowfires, sensual

Home Sweet Texas Home, Texas Home book one (sweet)

173

Caroline's Contemporary Mysteries:

Almost Home, a Link Dixon mystery

Death in the Garden, a Heather Cameron cozy mystery

Take Advantage of Bargain Boxed Sets:

Wild Western Women Ride Again, due to the success of the first boxed set, USA Today bestselling authors Kirsten Osbourne and Callie Hutton, and Amazon bestselling authors Sylvia McDaniel, Merry Farmer, and Caroline Clemmons offer another five novellas.

Wild Western Women, five western historical novellas by USA Today bestselling authors Kirsten Osbourne and Callie Hutton, and Amazon bestselling authors Sylvia McDaniel, Merry Farmer, and Caroline Clemmons, plus short stories by Merry Farmer and Caroline Clemmons.

Mail-Order Tangle, a western historical duet includes Mail-Order Promise by Caroline Clemmons and Mail-Order Ruckus by Jacquie Rogers.

Hearts and Flowers: Save Your Heart For Me, Happy Is The Bride, Long Way Home.

10 Timeless Heroes, time travels include Out Of The Blue and novels by Sky Purington, Skhye Moncreif, Donna Michaels, Beth Trissel, P. L. Parker, L. L. Muir, Linda LaRoque, and Nancy Lee Badger.

Men of Stone Mountain, offers the first three of the Stone Mountain Texas series at a reduced price: Brazos Bride, High Stakes Bride, and Bluebonnet Bride.

Rawhide n' Roses 2,000 word short stories by fifteen western authors introduce readers to their voice and style.

About the Author

Caroline Clemmons is an Amazon bestselling author of historical and contemporary western romances whose books have garnered numerous awards. Her latest release is O'NEILL'S TEXAS BRIDE, book two of her McClintock series. A frequent speaker at conferences and seminars, she has taught workshops on characterization, point of view, building a hero, and layering a novel.

Caroline is a member of Romance Writers of America (RWA) and the RWA chapters Yellow Rose, From The Heart, and Hearts Through History. Her latest publications include the acclaimed historical Men of Stone Mountain Texas series and the audio books of BRAZOS BRIDE and HIGH STAKES BRIDE. Her Kincaid series also remains popular with readers.

Caroline and her husband live in the heart of Texas cowboy country with their menagerie of rescued pets. Prior to writing full time, her jobs included stay-at-home mom (her favorite), secretary, newspaper reporter and featured columnist, assistant to the managing editor of a psychology journal, bookkeeper for the local tax assessor and—for a short and fun time—an antique dealer. When she's not indulging her passion for writing, Caroline enjoys family time, reading, travel, antiquing, genealogy, oil painting, and getting together with friends. Find her on her blog, website, Facebook, Twitter, Goodreads, and Pinterest.

Manufactured by Amazon.ca
Bolton, ON